Lovify
THE WORLD

Dr. Luv, RLM

The Quest to Lovify the World
Copyright © 2018 by Dr. Luv

All rights reserved. No part of this publication may be reproduced, distributed, or transmitted in any form or by any means, including photocopying, recording, or other electronic or mechanical methods, without the prior written permission of the author, except in the case of brief quotations embodied in critical reviews and certain other non-commercial uses permitted by copyright law.

Tellwell Talent
www.tellwell.ca

ISBN
978-0-2288-0033-0 (Hardcover)
978-0-2288-0032-3 (Paperback)
978-0-2288-0034-7 (eBook)

ACKNOWLEDGEMENTS

My sincere thanks to the following people for their help.

To my loving wife, and amazing family and friends, thank you for your love and support.

Jill Noelle, my angel editor, for breathing life into the story.

Dr. Anne Marie Evers for inspiring me to write when I was feeling ill.

Candice Mohn, for your timely intuition and insights.

Celeste and Joselyn Neyedli for your review and encouragement.

Kim, Rowan, and Kade for your input and unwavering support.

Nicolle Christie Bendheim for your review and for asking, "when can I read Book II?".

And to my son for reflecting your parent's love and for adopting your pop's golf lessons.

DEDICATION

To Jessie, although you left us too early, your
bright spirit shines on "I am Love".

In support of the West Coast Kid's Cancer Foundation.

WEEK 1

Daniel dragged his feet as he climbed the staircase toward the pediatric ward at the old, brick hospice building downtown. On each landing was a bank of windows overlooking the empty, wooded lot out back, and he paused in between the second and third floor to look out through the grimy, thin glass panes. A bit of movement caught his eye—someone or something in the scraggly brush—and he shivered. This place gave him the heebie-jeebies. Not only did the building have to be something like a hundred years old, but the surroundings were depressing—broken asphalt, overflowing dumpsters, and those untended, overgrown woods, where God-only-knew-what hid in the shadows.

Daniel would rather be anywhere else but there, he thought, as he continued his upward climb, moving super-slowly to kill some of the time he'd be forced to spend inside these dreary walls. Well, *almost* anywhere else. There *was* one other place he dreaded more, and coincidentally enough, his desire to avoid going back to that other place was exactly why he found himself at the hospice today...

Once Daniel reached the third floor, he pushed the bar across the door and entered an empty hallway. His tennis shoes squeaked on the linoleum as he took a left and headed down toward a room at the far end of the corridor, hoping he'd remembered the nurse's instructions on how to reach the little girl's room correctly.

312. The numbers were etched into a little black plaque on the wall outside the open door to the room. Daniel peeked inside, squinting at the small yet bright-eyed and big haired child sitting in the bed.

"What are you looking at? You look scared...like you just saw a ghost or something." The little girl in the bed giggled. "Maybe I do look a bit like a ghost, but I'm a friendly spirit, so please, come on in."

"Sorry," Daniel told her, embarrassed at being caught staring. He took a couple steps and came to a stop just inside the door. "I didn't mean to stare. I just didn't know if I had the right room. I'm looking for Angela, and I thought the nurse said room number 312."

The child giggled again. "You have the right room, but you might have the wrong girl. My name is Angel, but sometimes, the doctors and nurses call me Angela by mistake." She sighed and lay back against a mound of pillows that seemed to swallow her up, she was so tiny and thin. "So maybe you do have the right room after all. Who were you expecting to visit?"

"I don't know. I was ordered—I mean *asked* to pay a visit to a sick kid. They told me she was very, very sick. You don't look too ill, although you are very small; I mean, you're not what I was expecting. They said she would be in room 312, and I should be prepared for a shocking sight." Daniel snapped his mouth shut, wondering if he was saying too much. If this was the girl he was supposed to spend some time with, she might be offended or embarrassed by the description he'd been given.

"Well, sorry to disappoint you. I'm sorry I don't look shockingly sick enough for you. Here, maybe it'll help if I remove my wig." Angel reached up and pulled a mass of hair off her head. "Now do I look like a sick kid or a ghost perhaps?"

Daniel stared at her bald head, and his heart sank. He *had* hurt her feelings. "Oh, no, no I didn't mean to offend you. Please, put your hair—I mean your wig—back on."

"Why? Do I scare you? Don't you think I'm pretty?" She sat up again, turning her head this way and that, as if modeling her new look.

Daniel was silent for a moment while he studied her. To his surprise, he actually found her quite cute, with her big eyes and dimpled cheeks. "No," he told her, speaking the truth. "You don't scare me, and in fact, I think you're very pretty."

Angel threw back her head and laughed. The sound reminded Daniel of tiny, tinkling bells.

"Don't worry; it wasn't a test. I scared myself the first time I peeked in the mirror after... Seeing a kid staring back at me with no hair was weird at first, but it's kind of nice being bald." She laughed again. "I can wash my hair—I mean, my bald head—with just warm, soapy water and a cloth. Didn't they tell you I was a hairless kid?"

Daniel shook his head and leaned back against the block wall. "No, they didn't say anything about your hair—or your head. They just said you were very sick and that I should be prepared."

The little girl frowned, her brow lowering over those big blue eyes of hers. "Prepared for what? I don't bite, you know. Oh, except when they try sticking needles in my arm. Sometimes, I freak out, and I try to pinch and bite the nurses."

"Well, Angela, I would probably try pinching or biting a nurse, too, if they kept sticking needles in my arm." His gaze moved to her skinny limbs, and he could imagine how badly that would hurt her, with barely any flesh on her bones to add any cushion to a pinprick. The thought made his heart ache.

"Angel," she told him with a nod. "You should call me Angel. Why don't you come all the way inside my room, instead of standing like a guard at my door? You can sit in that chair, and maybe we can talk. I don't get many strangers visiting me, but I do get lots of family and friends stopping in. My mom and dad just left, and visiting hours are almost over. So, let's chat. What's your name?"

Daniel did as she requested, and as he settled into the vinyl-covered chair beside her bed, he said, "Daniel, my name is Daniel.

"Well, nice to meet you, Daniel."

She held out her hand as if to shake, but before he could respond, she pulled back.

"No, wait, can I call you Danny? You look like a Danny, and my hamster is called Danny-Boy, so I won't forget your name." She let loose another peel of her tinkling laughter.

Daniel couldn't help but smile, despite her silly suggestion. "Yeah, you can call me Danny. Heck, you can call me Danny-Boy, if you want."

The kid was sick, after all; if it made her happy to call him by the same name she used for her hamster…well, why not?

"Okay, Danny-Boy, it is!" She moved on the bed to face him, settling with her legs crisscrossed and watching him with an earnest expression.

"So…why are you here visiting a 'very sick kid'?" she asked, using the description he'd given her earlier.

Daniel had trouble meeting her intense gaze. Instead, he looked past her, over her shoulder to the pair of windows in the back wall. Did she have the same view he'd seen when he'd climbed the staircase to reach her floor? If so, he felt doubly sorry for her. Finally, he glanced at her face, and then looked down at his hands in his lap. "Well, it's a long story, but I just started volunteering at the hospice, and, well, they said I should come and visit you."

She was silent for a moment, almost as if she sensed he wasn't telling her the entire truth, but then she nodded. "I'm glad you did, Danny-Boy, and it's really nice to meet you. I'm seven years old, but I'm not supposed to make it to eight. How old are you?"

Daniel's mouth dropped open. Had he heard her correctly? "What did you just say?"

"I asked how old you are," she said, her tone patient, as if she were the young adult, and he was a small child.

"Sorry." Daniel shook his head. "I meant the other part. Did you just say you're not supposed to make it to eight?"

Angel nodded. "Yup. But that's okay. Don't look so sad. Eight is overrated, anyways, and I like being seven. So…how old are you?"

"I'm twenty-one," he told her, "but I don't understand. Why did you say you're not going to make it to eight?"

Angel lowered her gaze and fiddled with the tube of an IV that was taped to the inside of her arm. After a moment, she looked back up at him. "Because I'm a very sick kid, remember? My mom didn't want me to know, but I overheard my parents talking to the doctors. My mom and dad started to cry when the doc said I only have three months left to live. I guess the cancer is more serious than they told me." She paused, then added softly, "But that's okay."

"I'm sorry." Daniel cringed inwardly. Talk about lame. The kid had less than ninety days to live, and all he could think to say was "I'm sorry"?

"Why are you sorry? We just met, and you have nothing to be sorry about. Besides, there are younger kids than me who are very, very sick. At least, *I* can get up and walk around, and I have this pretty blonde wig to wear. Aren't I beautiful?"

Daniel nodded and forced a smile. "You are beautiful, and you are a very brave, young girl." Suddenly, his eyes started stinging, and he had a strong urge to run away. He got to his feet. "I have to go now, Angel."

"Wait, you can't leave yet." She stuck out her lower lip in an exaggerated pout. "You don't even know what my favorite color is."

But Daniel was already backing toward the door. "I really am sorry; I do have to go, but I can come back."

Her frown disappeared, and her eyes lit up. "When?" she asked him. "When can you visit me next?"

Daniel stuffed both hands into his pants pockets and shrugged. "They said I have to come… I mean, I can visit you once a week. I'll be back next Friday at about the same time. Is that okay?"

She nodded enthusiastically, obviously happy with his statement. "Yes, Danny-Boy, I look forward to our next visit. But do me a favor and please, try to come earlier. And I hope you look happier next time! If you bring me a big smile, I might let you try on my wig!" She giggled again.

"Thanks, Angela—oops! I mean *Angel*." He backed out into the hallway. "Good night, sweetie."

"Did you just call me sweetie?"

This time, she laughed hard, a true belly laugh that had Daniel blushing.

"I-I'm sorry…" he mumbled.

"That's okay. I didn't mean to embarrass you. I like it because I am a sweet, little Angel!" She waved at him from her spot in the middle of the bed. "Good night, Danny-Boy. Oh, I almost forgot to tell you what my favorite color is."

Daniel released a sigh. Would he ever get out of there? "What is it?" he asked, forcing himself to remain patient.

"It's red because red stands for love. Remember that, okay?"

"Okay, I will." He ran a hand through his hair then quickly dropped his hand to his side. "Thanks, Angel."

"If you need a reminder, wear something red, and see how you feel. You could pretend you're wearing your love!"

Wearing my love? Um… Daniel frowned. He didn't really understand this peculiar little girl, but he supposed if he had just three months to live, he might be a little odd, too. "Okay. Night, night. Sleep tight, and don't let the nurses bite!"

He turned and fled back down the linoleum-tiled hallway toward the steps, followed by the tinkling sound of Angel's laughter.

*****

As Daniel made his way down the cracked sidewalk toward the bus stop, his thoughts went to the events that had led him to that hospital room on the third floor of the old hospice building, where he'd met little Angel.

Daniel recalled the look on the judge's face as he'd stared down from the bench at Daniel and pronounced sentence. He'd felt as if the man had been peering into Daniel's soul as he'd listened to the price he'd have to pay for his criminal actions. Two years of incarceration, a year of probation, and two months of community service... At the time, Daniel had felt torn. While the verdict had sounded incredibly scary to him—especially the part about serving two years in prison!—on the other hand, as he'd listened to his mother cry and to the sobs from his victim's family members, Daniel had thought the punishment not nearly severe enough. How many lives had he screwed up with his stupid, thoughtless, negligent actions? As the bailiff had placed him in handcuffs and led him through a back door in the courtroom to take him to begin serving his sentence, Daniel had hung his head in shame, unable to look any of the people he'd harmed in the eye.

The two years he'd spent behind bars had been by far the scariest time in his young-adult life. The only things that had kept him sane were the weekly visits from his distraught mother. He'd tried to wear a brave face each time she'd come to see him, and his heart had ached, as he'd listened to her pour out her apologies for being a struggling, single mom. She had even apologized for Daniel's absent, deadbeat dad. Daniel hated hearing her talk that way. As far as he was concerned, he had the best mom on the planet, and she'd done the best she could to raise him up right. He felt her pain, he'd heard her disappointment, but he'd also sensed her unwavering love and support. For that, he could never repay her or thank her enough... But if it was the last thing he did, he'd make her proud of him.

Upon his release from prison, Daniel had tried to prepare himself emotionally for the court-ordered community service. The veteran judge must have had a sound reason for sending Daniel to work with a sick little girl who had just three months to live, but as the city bus came to a stop on the corner, and Daniel and two other passengers climbed on board, he hadn't a clue what that reason might be. The child—Angel—was around the same age as—

Daniel shook his head, dismissing that thought. The last thing he needed was to break down crying on a bus full of other passengers...

Bad enough he'd carried his guilt and shame into the hospice the other day when he'd gone to sign up for service. The hospice staff had eyed him suspiciously, and they'd questioned the judge's motive for assigning this particular line of the community service. Sending Daniel to the sick children's hospital had not seemed like the appropriate punishment for his crime. But Daniel hadn't been able to answer their questions about the judge's motives, and in the end, they'd assigned him to visit a child they called "Angela," whom he'd have to visit every day for the next seven weeks.

Angela—aka Angel—had come as a surprise to Daniel. He hadn't expected to meet such an energetic and spunky kid. He was still surprised by how...*healthy* she seemed, considering she didn't have long to live. He'd also assumed his punishment would be uncomfortable and boring. But after meeting Angel, he could tell this experience was going to be anything but boring. He had made it through the first visit with his emotions in check—barely—and without revealing any of the sordid details of his past. Daniel had seven weeks to go, and he was determined to make it through with his emotions intact.

WEEK 2

Daniel would have given anything to turn back the clock and do things differently, but life didn't work that way, and nothing was ever that easy. He had made a terrible mistake that had altered or destroyed several lives—his, his victim's, his family's and hers... All those poor, innocent people, impacted by his negligent actions. As Daniel dragged himself down the hallway toward Angel's room that second Friday, he could still hear the judge's harsh reprimand echoing in his mind.

"Young man," the judge had said, "I hope you learn how precious life is!"

As he neared room 312, Daniel tried to forget about the past and focus on his visit with Angel. He wasn't sure what to expect this time. He hoped for another quick visit and, hopefully, one with fewer prying questions—questions that made him uncomfortable and, frankly, scared him a little bit.

"Angel, Angel, are you sleeping?" he asked softly as he stepped into her dimly lit room. Didn't they ever turn on all the lights around there? The old building was gloomy enough without the added shadows caused by low-watt bulbs, most of which didn't seem to be lit. "I don't want to disturb you. I can come back later if you like."

"Hello, who's there? Is that you, Danny-Boy? Come on in," she said, "and please don't mind my sleepy voice. The nurses told me the medication would make me feel tired, and it might give me an upset tummy, too, and they were right."

Daniel frowned and stepped farther into the room. Still, he hesitated to approach the bed. If Angel was sick, she probably wasn't in the mood for company. "Is your tummy upset now? Can I get you some water or juice or something?"

"No." Angel sighed and scrunched up her cute, little button nose. "No more water or juice." She cleared her froggy throat and continued. "You know what I'd really love? A strawberry milkshake with whipped cream and a fresh strawberry on top!"

She giggled, that sweet sound Daniel had begun to associate with the little girl, such a contrast to how she appeared.

"Don't look so surprised, Danny-Boy. My dad used to take me for a strawberry milkshake every Friday night. It is Friday night, isn't it?"

"Yes, it is, but I don't know where I can get you a strawberry milkshake. Do they have milkshakes in the cafeteria?" He started to turn, thinking he'd go in search of the cafeteria and get Angel her treat.

"No, I'm afraid they only sell boring drinks like juice and milk. I get juice three times a day with my medication. It's supposed to help calm my tummy. Can you please pass me my apple juice?" She nodded toward the table next to her bed, upon which sat a Styrofoam cup with a straw sticking out of the lid, surrounded by at least a half-dozen beautiful cards.

"Wow, Angel," he said, as he rounded her bed and picked up the cup. "You've received a lot of cards and gifts."

In addition to the cards, there were several stuffed animals, a small stack of children's books, and a couple boxes that contained what looked like board games of some kind.

"I know," she told him, accepting the cup of juice he handed her. She nodded and took a long pull on the straw before she continued. "My family and friends have spoiled me. The nurses had to take away most of the flowers, but they left the cards and other gifts, and of course, my special, cute friend, Red."

"Red?" Daniel eyed the pile of gifts on the table. "Who's Red?"

"He's the teddy bear with the pretty red bow. My grandmother gave him to me. I named him Red, and I just love him to pieces." She pointed to the bear sitting in the middle of a group of other stuffed animals. "You can hold him if you want to. He's really soft and cuddly, and he makes me feel better when I'm sick."

Daniel picked up the little brown bear with his gigantic red bow and turned him in his hands. "He's cute, Angel."

"Did you have a special stuffed animal when you were a kid, Danny-Boy?" She took another sip of her juice and eyed him innocently over the lid of the cup.

Daniel closed his eyes a moment as he dealt with the memory evoked by Angel's innocent question. Finally, he nodded. "I did, actually, but that was a long time ago."

"What was his name?" She turned in the bed to face him, obviously intent on grilling him about his long-ago, most-favorite stuffed buddy.

Daniel set Red back in his spot on the table, avoiding Angel's penetrating gaze. "It doesn't matter," he told her. *Please drop the subject...please...*

But obviously, Angel wasn't about to give up so easily. "It matters to me. Come on, Danny-Boy, what did you call him?"

Daniel heaved a sigh. "*She* was called Sox." He met Angel's gaze.

"You had a girl teddy bear, and you called her Sox?" She giggled, but when he didn't return her smile, she put a hand over her mouth and shook her head. "Sorry..."

Daniel frowned and looked down at his feet. The same worn linoleum covered the floor in her room, scratched and yellowed by years of wear and tear. He really didn't like talking about this stuff and wished he could somehow avoid answering or change the subject. How could such a young girl make him feel so...vulnerable? Finally, he sucked in a breath and looked back up at her. "No, she wasn't a teddy bear."

Angel leaned toward him. "Well then, what kind of stuffed animal was she, Danny-Boy?"

He paused. Once he told her, she'd probably laugh her head off. He tried to steel himself for her inevitable teasing. "She was a sock. I mean, she was a sock *puppet*. My grandmother made her for me. I think she thought I was lonely because I didn't have any brothers or sisters. Sox made me feel better when I was feeling sick or sad, just like Red makes *you* feel better."

"A sock puppet called Sox? How original is that?"

Daniel tamped down his rising irritation. "I didn't know what else to call her. Besides, I thought Sox was a great name, and so did my mom and grandmother." He recognized the defensiveness in his voice, but he couldn't seem to help himself.

"Okay, okay." Angel held her hands up in a placating gesture. "Don't get upset. If I can call my teddy bear Red just because he has a red bow, then you can call your pet sock Sox."

"She wasn't my pet. She was a special gift from my grandmother, and she was cute." He lifted his chin a little.

"Did you love her?"

Daniel stared, her question catching him off guard. "Love who, my grandmother? Of course!"

"Yes, of course, you loved your grandmother, Daniel; everyone loves their grandmother! I meant, did you love Sox?"

"What? No. I mean, yeah, I guess so. I don't know. It was the only thing that I kept from childhood. All my toys and stuffed animals got donated when I moved out."

"You still have her? That's totally awesome! But, Danny-Boy, you just called Sox an it. Does that mean you don't love her anymore?"

Daniel made a noise that signaled his impatience. "I guess I still love her, but why are you asking me these silly questions?" He started edging toward the door. Maybe it was time to bring this visit to an end. This little trip down Memory Lane had gotten under his skin, and suddenly, he wanted to be alone so he could examine what it was about the conversation that bothered him so badly.

"It's a test, Daniel, and you'll discover why later. Right now, I need my apple juice, or preferably a strawberry shake if you have one in your back pocket." She grinned, and those cute little dimples of hers appeared on her cheeks.

"Sorry, Angel," he said, thankful she'd changed the subject but wondering what she'd meant by her question being a "test." "It must have fallen out on the way over here. Or maybe Sox drank your milkshake?" He winked.

"Yeah, I bet that's exactly what happened!"

Daniel took a good look at her, noting the dark circles beneath her sunken eyes and her skinny arms. She was bone-thin, and he wondered if the hospice was feeding her enough or if her illness was entirely to blame for her thin physique. "If you really need a milkshake, I could go get you one. I think there's a fast-food place down on the next block." He took another step toward the door.

"No, I'm okay. But thanks, Danny-Boy. That's really sweet of you. The apple juice is fine." She reached over and grabbed the Styrofoam cup off her little side table. "But I am a little disappointed in you." She gave him an exaggerated pout. "You haven't said one word about my hair yet."

Daniel studied her wig—the same one she'd had on last Friday. "It was the first thing I noticed when I walked in the room," he said, figuring one little white lie wouldn't hurt; especially if it made her feel good. "It looks really nice, but why did you add a red streak?" He grinned. "Did you want to look more like your teddy bear?"

Angel giggled. "No, smarty-pants. If you recall, red is my favorite color, and since it represents love, I thought, why not add some red to my beautiful blonde wig?" She turned her head this way and that. "It does look lovely, doesn't it? By the way, how come you're not wearing any red? Not feeling the love this week, Danny-Boy? Did you and Sox have a falling out?"

Danny sighed. "Now who's acting like a smarty-pants? I'll try to remember to wear something red next week. Maybe I'll even wear a red bow. That is, if Red doesn't mind?" He shook his head over their silly bantering then glanced up at the big, round clock on the wall above the door. "Well, I guess I should get going, and let you get some rest. You look tired this week, Angel."

"Aw, don't go yet. You just got here, and I could use some company. It helps take my mind off my upset tummy. Can you come closer, and help me sit up, please?"

Daniel hesitated just a moment. He had another thirty minutes before the bus came, and if he didn't spend that time with Angel, he'd be stuck sitting on the bench at the bus stop, and the temperature had dropped considerably in the last twenty-four hours.

He shrugged and returned to Angel's bedside. "How do we do this?" he asked her. "I don't want to hurt you." She looked so fragile, as if she might break if he weren't super careful.

She held out both arms. "Here. Just take my hands, and pull me up. But do it slowly. My stomach hasn't been feeling too great again tonight."

He gently lifted her frail body, and with one hand on her shoulder to keep her upright, he carefully tucked a large pillow behind her bony back. He hadn't expected to stay this long or to get this close. He wasn't comfortable offering support to a sick kid—or any kid, for that matter. His guilt was etched too deeply into his heart.

"If you stay a little longer, I'll tell you all about my cancer. That is, if you're interested?"

Again, Daniel hesitated. He'd been curious about Angel's sickness from the moment he'd met her, but could he handle hearing all the so-called gory details? More importantly, could Angel handle talking about it? For such a young girl, she seemed very…*mature* sometimes. He crossed to the windows along the back wall of her room and looked out. As he'd guessed the prior week, her room did look overlook the rear parking area and the wooded lot. How depressing. "Yes," he said finally and turned around. "I'm interested. I can't imagine what you're going through. You're so young, and it just doesn't seem fair. But are you sure you want to talk about this? We don't have to, you know?"

"Well, I agree it doesn't seem fair, especially since my cancer is very rare. About a year ago, I was diagnosed with metastatic pineoblastoma. I know…it sounds like a great name for a heavy metal band, doesn't it?" She flashed him a smile. "But unfortunately, it doesn't have a very good encore. Pineoblastomas are rare and aggressive tumors that mainly crop up in kids my age. These child-attacking tumors originate in the pineal gland, and they are treated primarily with radiation and chemotherapy. The pediatric oncologist said I needed high doses of chemo to treat my malignant brain tumor. Maybe that's why I look like a ghost."

"I never said you looked like a ghost," he reminded her. "You're the one who said that, remember?" Before she could answer, he shook his head and went on. "Wow, Angel, did your doctor tell you all that stuff about your diagnosis?" He couldn't imagine any adult sharing that kind of information with a little kid.

But Angel shook her head. "Nope, I learned about cancer all by myself. Although, I didn't know about the terminal part until I overheard the doctor and my parents talking." She started messing with her IV tube again. "To be honest, that scared me at first, but I've accepted it now. I only wish my parents could accept it, too. I can usually hear them sobbing when they leave my room. It's been three months since the diagnosis. According to the National Institute of Health, the likelihood that a patient will survive for long after a diagnosis is not high. The doctor gave me six months to live, so I guess I can understand why my parents are so upset." She spoke softly but with an underlying strength in her voice.

"You sound so mature talking about this," he told her. And she really did, too. If Daniel didn't know better, he'd think she was at least three times her age. Like an old soul in a young girl's body. "How does a seven-year-old kid know so much about this rare cancer? Did the nurses share their knowledge with you?"

"I guess you could say I'm smart for my age." She looked up at him and grinned. "Plus, I know how to operate an iPad, I have free Wi-Fi, and I have lots of spare time on my hands. So, I can search and learn about all kinds of interesting topics."

"You've been doing your own cancer research online?" Daniel didn't know whether to be impressed or depressed by her admission. While other seven-year-old kids were doing…whatever little kids did these days, Angel was reading all about a disease that was going to kill her within weeks. The thought saddened him in a way that frightened him.

"Yup, when I was admitted to this hospital, my mom gave me a pretty pink iPad, and I call her Pinky. It was supposed to be a secret because Mom knew my dad wouldn't approve. He's old-school, and he thinks kids spend too much time on their electronic gadgets and not enough time playing outside. News flash for my dad; I can't go play outside. My mom is more understanding, and she knew I would go crazy if I didn't have something to entertain my busy, little mind. She only had a few hard rules for using my iPad, and, unfortunately, I broke one of them during the first week."

Daniel raised a brow. For some reason, he could believe that, and his curiosity got the better of him. "Why? What did you do?"

Angel shrugged. "Well, Mom was pretty clear that I could connect to the Wi-Fi, as long as I didn't post anything on social media sites or search inappropriate topics or do anything that would get me into trouble. The last rule was a challenge for me, and my love for pizza cost me two weeks without Pinky!"

Daniel shook his head, thoroughly confused. "Wow, how did you get into trouble with Pinky and a pizza?"

"Have you tried the food in this place, Danny-Boy?" Angel faked an elaborate shiver. "It's disgusting, especially for a very sick kid with tainted taste buds! One night, I was hungry and frustrated with the awful-tasting rice pudding, so I Googled pizza parlors in the area. I ended up chatting online with a sympathetic pizza clerk. I tried to order a large pepperoni and cheese pizza, and everything was going along fine until Pedro asked for a credit card number. To get that close to completing an order is sheer torture, so I pulled out the sympathy, cancer-kid card." She paused and drew in a deep breath before telling him the rest. "About thirty minutes later—faster delivery time than was stated on their website—an eager-looking, pizza-delivery guy showed up at the back entrance with four complimentary…that's right, four *free*, large, cheese-and-pepperoni pizzas and two large bottles of pop! A friend in room 303 helped me sneak the pizzas and pop into the playroom, and me and the other kids had a feast. We even delivered slices of pizza to the kids who couldn't get out of their sick beds."

Daniel chuckled, unable to hide his amusement. Now *that* sounded like something a little kid would do. "So, what happened? Why did you get into so much trouble?"

"Well, it didn't take long for the spicy pizza smells to make the rounds past the nursing station. They went into full alert; I think it was called a code red? They quickly found the source of the pizza smells and the culprit kids with the sauce stains on our sterile hospital gowns. The nurses were scrambling like mice, sniffing out the cheese in all the rooms with the immobile kids."

Daniel shook his head. "I still don't get it. All kids love pizza. What was the big deal?"

"Oh, Danny-Boy, that's what I thought, too, but the chaos I'd caused was just getting started. I discovered that cheese and spicy pepperoni doesn't mix well with sick kids and all of our medications. It didn't take long for the digestive reactions to erupt, and before you could say vomit and diarrhea, every available nurse and all the cleaning staff were scouring our rooms for sick kids and sick symptoms! They were running around emptying bed pans, scrubbing toilets, and reassuring kids that the pizza wasn't poisoned! One grouchy, old nurse scolded me for causing all that trouble and for putting other kids at risk. I felt like I was being punished from the inside out, because my tummy ejected the three pieces of delicious pizza, too."

For a moment, Daniel thought Angel might cry; she looked so forlorn. Without thinking, he reached out and patted her hand.

"It was a long, smelly, and scary night. I felt sorry for the white-faced kids and the exhausted nurses and janitors. Everyone was okay by morning, but that was before the parents showed up for visiting. My punishment was swift. My mom banned me from using Pinky for two weeks, and my dad just shook his head in disbelief and disappointment. I think he was angrier at my mom for getting me an iPad to begin with, especially since he didn't know about it. I even got the pizza delivery guy in trouble, too. They said he should have known better than to deliver pizzas to a hospital floor full of sick kids. I felt sorry for him, and I explained to my mom and dad and the nurses that it was all my fault!"

Despite Angel's obvious agony over what had occurred, Daniel was having a hard time hiding his amusement. His lips twitched, and before he could stop himself, he let out a loud, joyous peel of laughter.

Angel scowled. "Are you laughing at me, Danny-Boy? You think my poisoned-pizza story is funny?"

Daniel sucked in a deep breath and tried to be sober. "Sorry, Angel, I don't mean to make fun of what happened."

Her scowl disappeared and she grinned. "Oh, that's okay. Everyone survived, and now that I think about it, it was like a crazy scene out of a kid's comedy movie." She paused and gave him a searching look. "It's nice to see you laughing. I have a feeling you needed a good laugh."

Once again, Daniel marveled at her insightfulness for such a young girl. "You're right," he admitted. "I guess I haven't been feeling very happy lately."

Her expression turned serious. "Why? Did something happen to you?"

Daniel stiffened. "Yeah, but I don't feel like talking about it. I did something very bad, and I deserve to feel this way."

Angel huffed. "Nobody *deserves* to feel sad or guilty, Danny-Boy. No matter what happened, you have to let it go."

He shook his head. She didn't understand, but then again, how could she? And he wasn't about to try to explain. Not now...probably not ever. "You don't get it," he told her. "It's not that easy. I did something terrible, and I have to live with it for the rest of my life. I don't expect a seven-year-old kid to understand."

"What if you only had three months to live? What would you do then? Life is too short to carry burdens, guilt, and sadness in your heart. Whatever you did, you have to forgive yourself. Forgiveness is the first step to loving yourself, and if you can't love yourself unconditionally, how can you love others unconditionally?"

He gave her a lop-sided smile, amused by her philosophical attitude. "Wow, Angel, where did that bit of wisdom come from? Did you find that online, too?"

"Well, yes, I did, actually. I was searching for natural cancer cures, and I came across some very interesting information about the power of love for healing. Did you know that researchers have been measuring the positive effects of love on the body, mind, and emotions? Imagine if we could heal ourselves, heal each other, and heal the planet, too, with love! What would our world be like if everyone embraced unconditional puppy love, Danny-Boy?"

Unconditional puppy love? She was sounding her age again, and possibly a wee bit naïve. "You're right; our world definitely needs more love. Maybe the nurses and janitors needed to feel the love on pizza night."

"Funny, Danny-Boy, very funny. I don't think they were feeling the love that night!" Her expression grew serious again. "How about you, Daniel, are you feeling the love? Self-love, that is."

He shook his head, sighed, and glanced back out the windows. "No, like I mentioned, it's very complicated." He turned back to Angel and forced a smile. "Anyway, it's getting late, and I should get going, and you should get some rest. I had a nice time visiting with you tonight, and I really appreciate your funny pizza story. You have a gift for making people feel better. I'm sorry for not being very cheerful company for you."

Angel slumped back against the pillows. "Oh, Daniel, you're great company. You're a good listener, and I feel as if we're destined to become close friends." She flashed a grin. "Maybe Red and Sox will become friends, too?"

Daniel chuckled. "That would be a match made in baseball heaven. People could call them the Red-Sox couple!" He wondered if she'd even understand the reference.

"Funny, Danny-Boy, but my teddy bear does not like baseball. Red loves football and soccer."

Once again, she surprised him with her knowledge. Was there anything this seven-year-old little girl *didn't* know about? "Oh, well," he told her. "That's too bad. I guess Red and Sox will just remain acquaintances, but

I'm happy to be your friend. You're a cool kid, and you're wise way beyond your years."

Angel laughed her sweet laugh. "Thanks to Pinky and the Internet, I'm learning a lot about love and life. Speaking of which… I learned really quick that a seven-year-old kid has to be pretty careful when Googling the word *love*. My mom and dad would be shocked at the number of times I had to hit delete, delete, delete!"

Daniel straightened. He crossed his arms and gave Angel a stern look. "You better be careful. The world can be a dark and scary place sometimes. Especially online! There are all kinds of creepy things—and people—on the web!"

She nodded. "I know. Believe me, I know, and I'll be careful. Promise." She sighed and glanced up at the clock. "I guess you have to go, but before you do, would you do me a big favor?"

"Sure, anything for my sweet Angel."

"Aww, you called me a sweet Angel. That's very nice, Danny-Boy. I knew from the moment we met that you were hiding a deep, dark secret, and tonight you confirmed you've been suffering for a while. I asked you earlier what you would do if you only had three months left to live. I don't need an answer tonight, but I would really appreciate it if you would do something for me and for yourself."

Daniel hesitated. This line of conversation made him uncomfortable, but he really did need to get out of there, and he figured it would be quicker to just find out what she wanted him to do and agree to do it. "Okay, Angel, you have my curious-cat whiskers going. What is it?"

"Your curious-cat whiskers?" Angel giggled. "That's cute. Do you like animals, Daniel?"

"Yes, I grew up with cats, and they were always inquisitive, curious, and mischievous." *Kind of like you,* he thought, and smiled. "That's why I made the curious-cat whiskers comment." He edged toward the door. He really didn't want to miss the bus. "So, what do you want me to do?"

Her expression turned dead serious. "Daniel, do you trust me?"

He thought about that for a moment and then nodded. "Yes, Angel, as weird as it sounds, I trust a seven-year-old kid who has natural, cat-like curiosity, a teddy bear called Red, and an iPad called Pinky."

"Okay, well, my cat senses are telling me you have to forgive yourself before you can ever love again. Does that make sense?" she asked.

"In a weird way, yes, it does." He nodded. She'd said something similar earlier, and her words had struck a nerve and had started him thinking. "It wouldn't be easy for me to forgive myself, though. Still, sometimes, I think I'd be willing to try almost anything to shake these sad feelings." He avoided her penetrating gaze, suddenly embarrassed. He wasn't used to talking about these things. Not with anyone. He glanced at the clock again.

"Awesome!" Angel clapped enthusiastically. "Then I have something fun and maybe a bit weird for you to try over this next week. Every time your thoughts drift to sadness or guilt or shame, repeat the following statement: I am love, and I forgive and love myself. It's easy; just repeat these words anytime you're feeling down or sad. It's something I learned online, and according to what I read, these positive affirmations, also known as Luvffirmations, work wonders for the body, mind, and soul. Will you try it, Danny-Boy? Please, say yes!"

She sounded a little like a scientist encouraging her newest guinea pig. The thought made Daniel chuckle. Plus, how could he say no to such a cute kid? "I'll be honest with you, Angel; it does sound a bit weird to me, but if it'll make you happy, I'll give it a try."

"Yay!" Angel clapped again and bounced up and down a little on her bed, causing the old springs to squeak. "Thank you, Danny-Boy. Have a great week. I'm already looking forward to our next visit!" She paused, then added, "Love you, Daniel."

Daniel's cheeks grew warm, and he ducked his head. "Oh…um, okay, thanks, Angel. See you next week. Um, do you need anything before I go?"

"Yeah, where is that strawberry milkshake?"

Daniel shook his head and laughed. "Funny, Angel. Very funny." He stepped out the door. "Good night," he called out over his shoulder, "and don't let the Red Sox bite!"

Daniel walked down the corridor toward the stairs with a spring in his step that hadn't been there in quite a while. For the first time in a couple of years, his spirits were lifted. Before tonight, he couldn't remember the last time he'd actually laughed.

As he pushed open the door leading to the back stairwell, he pictured Angel, sitting in the middle of her bed, grinning up at him. She was like a little, glowing...well, *angel*, and she seemed to have an uncanny ability to look past his façade and see his sorrow. He was a little concerned about all the questions she asked him, and he had to be careful he didn't say too much. Not only did he need to protect himself, but she didn't need to know any of the gruesome details about the past couple years. He'd come to think of that time as a dark chapter in his life, and he was trying to turn the page to a new beginning. But what Angel had said about loving himself made sense. His guilt was holding him back, and he was willing to try just about anything to shed those weighted feelings. Even Angel's suggestion that he repeat those words to himself all the time. What were they again? Oh, yeah...

"I am love, and I forgive and love myself."

As Daniel exited the back door of the hospice building, he heaved a sigh, and his breath made a huge puff of steam in the icy-cold air. He stuffed his hands into his coat pockets and ducked his head against the cold breeze.

I forgive and love myself... Daniel scoffed as the words floated through his mind. He'd never thought about forgiving *himself*; in fact, he'd done just the opposite. He'd always told himself he didn't deserve to be forgiven... or loved, for that matter.

****

Over the course of the following week, Daniel went through the motions, just as he had since being released from prison a short time ago. He went to work at his mindless job at the call center, and he went home every night to his boring, basement apartment. He was leading the lifeless life of an ex-convict, but he was okay with his mundane existence. He figured he deserved exactly what he had at the moment. After all, the people he'd hurt were no doubt still suffering. Why should he have it any better than they did? He was hiding from life, even avoiding his mother's repeated invitations to come over for a home-cooked meal. But the one thing he couldn't shut out was the favor Angel had asked of him—the advice she'd given him—and every once in a while, he would say those words in his head or whisper them under his breath. "I am love, and I forgive and love myself."

Daniel had heard of positive affirmations, even before Angel had brought up the subject during their last visit, but he'd always thought that kind of stuff was for hippies and new-age gurus. Still, science had proven that the mind was a powerful tool… He'd felt awkward, talking to himself like that—at least at first—but something told him Angel had a point. He had to break the bad habit of all the negative thoughts and self-talk he'd indulged in over the past couple years. He'd been spending a lot of time beating himself up and putting himself down, especially after he'd committed the biggest mistake of his life. But this week, he'd tried to remember to do things differently. Each time a negative thought entered his mind, he'd replace it with "I am love, and I forgive and love myself." It was too early to know for certain if this "Luvffirmation" would do him any lasting good, but by the end of the week, he was aware of a subtle shift in his feelings. He was looking forward to sharing his progress with Angel.

****

The sound of an obnoxious alarm awoke Daniel abruptly from a deep sleep. It was early Friday morning, and he sprang out of bed, ready to face the world.

"Today is going to be a good day," he told himself as he dressed for work.

After a half-mile walk and two bus transfers, Daniel arrived at the office fifteen minutes early. He waved at his supervisor, chuckling under his breath at the shocked look on the older man's face. Daniel had earned the reputation of being a sad, moody loner. For the most part, people had learned to leave him alone, so he could imagine how surprised his boss and coworkers were when he smiled and nodded greetings as he made his way to his little cubicle.

Over the last few weeks of working there, he'd heard the rumors and the whispering comments behind his back. They knew he was on probation, and from his first day on the job, his coworkers had seemed to find pleasure in shooting scathing looks his way. He'd felt like he had a target on his back, as if he was trapped in a schoolyard with a bunch of high school bullies. Although he'd never been physically attacked, their silent harassment had hurt him deeply. He'd rarely engaged in any meaningful or friendly conversations, but today, he'd decided things would be different.

He walked into the coffee room with his head held a little higher, and he greeted his co-workers with sincere and friendly good mornings. They responded with surprised looks, at first, and some seemed suspicious, as if they expected he had some ulterior motive, but after a minute or so, they acknowledged his greetings, and a few even smiled and said hello.

Daniel returned to his gray-walled cubicle, filled with a renewed sense of joy and a slightly adjusted view of life. He couldn't wait for the day to end so he could take the bus to the hospice and visit Angel. Just the thought of her smile when he told her about his experience with her *Luvffirmation* made him happy, and he decided he'd do something special for her. He wanted to thank her, and he knew exactly what to do to show her how much he appreciated her.

WEEK 3

"Angel, Angel, sweetie, I have a surprise for you," Daniel called out in a sing-song voice.

He peeked into her room, a bit disappointed to see her lights off and her motionless body tucked under the blankets. He crept across the linoleum-tiled floor until he reached her bed, then he touched her shoulder lightly.

"Angel," he whispered. "Hey, kiddo, wake up."

She stirred, and her eyelids flickered. She woke slowly, her gaze moving from his face to the cardboard drink tray he held in his hand, then back again. Her expression turned from sleepy to excited in a flash.

"Danny-Boy!" she said, her words laced with enthusiastic anticipation. "Is that what I think it is?" She scrambled to sit upright.

Daniel laughed and gently helped her get propped up with her pillows behind her back. "Yes, sweetie, it is. I have two strawberry milkshakes, one for you and one for me."

"Oh, Danny-Boy, you're the sweetest friend, ever!" She nodded toward the chair beside the bed. "Why don't you pull up a seat, and we can visit for a little while? But please, don't turn on the lights yet. My eyes are still snoozing, and I want to enjoy the delicious strawberry smell."

Daniel dragged the vinyl-covered chair closer to Angel's bedside, handed over her milkshake, then sat back in the chair, propping his tennis-shoe-clad feet on the bedrail. For a while, they sat in silence and sipped on their shakes. Angel made slurping sounds of appreciation, and every once in a while, she'd moan her delight.

Daniel chuckled softly. Her obvious gratitude gave him a warm feeling in the middle of his chest. Doing something nice for the little girl—making her happy—brought him a special kind of pleasure he couldn't ever remember experiencing. In fact, he probably felt just as happy about bringing her a milkshake as she did about receiving one.

Odd, he thought… He'd only known Angel for a couple weeks, but he felt a special bond with her. She was like a long-lost kid sister, a little girl he'd never met but one his heart had recognized and loved…instantly.

Angel finally broke the silence with a very loud slurp that signaled the bottom of the cup and her total satisfaction with her strawberry milkshake. Daniel laughed and made his own slurping sounds, topped off with a loud, bubbling burp. They both broke out in fits of laughter.

"What's going on in there?"

Both Daniel and Angel sobered immediately, and Angel stuffed her empty shake cup under her blanket, while Daniel held his down beside his chair, out of sight of the nurse who had stopped in the doorway to look inside the room.

"Is everything okay in here?" she asked, squinting in their direction.

"Um, yes," Angel said quickly. "We're fine. My friend Daniel and I were just laughing over a funny joke he told me."

The nurse frowned. "Well, keep it down a little bit. The boy in the next room isn't feeling too well tonight, and he's trying to sleep."

"Yes, Nurse Brown," Angel said solemnly.

"Yes, ma'am," Daniel said.

The nurse smiled and nodded before she continued down the hall.

As soon as the squish-squish sound of her soft-soled shoes on the tile floor could no longer be heard, Angel turned to Daniel.

"Robbie—he's the kid next door—has lymphoma," she said, her voice barely above a whisper. "I heard Nurse Brown and one of the other nurses talking the other day, and I think Robbie might be gone soon."

Daniel's stomach tightened painfully. "Gone? What do you mean?" he asked. Although he was pretty certain he knew the answer, he was hoping she'd say the kid would be going home soon.

"I think they've given him less time than they gave me."

The pain in Daniel's stomach grew worse. "I'm sorry, Angel. Is he a friend of yours?"

Angel shrugged. "We're all kind of in the same boat around here, so we've naturally grown close. Robbie is two years older than me, but yeah… we're friends." She straightened suddenly and drew a deep breath. "Anyway, thank you, Danny-Boy, for making my day." She grinned. "I forgot how much I loved strawberry milkshakes. The nurses have been disguising my daily medication in an artificial-strawberry flavor that smells like rotting berries and tastes like chalk. My taste buds and tummy are so thankful right now."

Daniel chuckled. Although he still felt badly for the little guy next door, he marveled at Angel's resiliency under such messed-up conditions. Seeing her smile again made him happy. "You're welcome, and to be honest, I think I enjoyed my milkshake as much as you enjoyed yours." A horrible thought occurred to him, and he groaned and put his face in his hands.

"What's wrong?" Angel asked. "Are you okay?"

"I just remembered what happened after your impromptu pizza party," he said, looking up at the feel of her hand on his arm. "You're not going to get sick, are you? Or get into trouble for me bringing you something that's not on the hospital's menu?"

Angel laughed her tinkling laugh. "No, Danny-Boy, you won't get me into trouble, and my stomach feels better now than it has in for-*ever*." She batted her eyelashes. "Besides, *I'm* just an innocent, sick kid who happens to love strawberry milkshakes. *You*, on the other hand, might get into *big* trouble if the nurses catch you sneaking in outside treats."

"Hmm," Daniel said, enjoying the teasing glint in her eyes. "Then maybe I shouldn't take such big chances. After all, I wouldn't want to get into *big* trouble…"

Angel frowned, obviously having realized her attempt at scaring him had backfired. "I really don't think it's necessary to go that far," she told him. "I mean, as long as we're careful, we shouldn't get caught, right?"

Daniel laughed. He'd already decided to bring his new little friend a strawberry shake every Friday night. The sight of her delighted smile was well worth the risk. "Don't worry; I'll be careful, Angel, and our illegal treats will remain our little secret. Heck, we could even come up with a code word if you want to—that way, if any of the nurses overhear us talking, they won't know what we mean."

"That's a great idea!" Angel sat up on her bed and leaned forward, a look of concentration on her face. "Hmm. What should we use? Berries? I know! Once we pick a code word, I can email you during the week, and if I want you to bring a milkshake with you to your Friday visits, I can put the code word in the subject line."

Daniel looked down at his empty milkshake cup and moved the straw in and out through the hole in the top of the lid. "No…I'm afraid that won't work. You can't contact me by email."

Angel frowned. "Sure, I can. I have my iPad, and my mom allowed me to set up an email account so I could keep in touch with some of my distant family and friends. She wouldn't let me connect through Facebook or any of those kinds of sites, and my dad doesn't approve of seven-year-olds using cellphones. So, the only way I can contact you is through email."

Daniel bit his lip and shook his head. "Um, you don't understand. No one can contact me through email because I don't have access to an email account or social media…or even a cellular network for that matter." Daniel still couldn't meet Angel's eyes. The last thing he wanted to do was face her inevitable questions about why he'd been cut off from anything remotely connected to the Internet and cellphones.

"What? Are you kidding me? How does a twenty-one-year-old guy survive without being connected? Are you anti-technology, or have you chosen to lead a sheltered life?"

He could feel her intense, curious stare, and he finally looked up at her.

"It's complicated," he mumbled, "but no, I am not anti-technology. In fact, in my former job, I was considered a tech wiz by my employer. I'm just… taking a break from technology for a little while." *Now please, let it go…*

But his ever-inquisitive little Angel shook her head. "Oh, Daniel, if we're going to be friends, you have to be honest with me. Let me guess—your self-imposed technology ban has something to do with that deep, dark secret of yours, right?"

Cheeks hot and no doubt as red as over-ripe tomatoes, Daniel glanced up at the clock above the door. "Maybe it's time for me to go."

"Oh, no, you don't! We've been sitting here chatting in the dark, and now you're trying to keep me in the dark. What's up?"

Daniel sighed. It wasn't so much that he wanted to keep the truth from her, but he hated the thought that she might think less of him if he told her. "Like I said last week, I really don't want to talk about it." He made an effort to soften his tone. He didn't want to hurt her feelings. "Can you please respect my wishes? Maybe we could talk about something else? How are your mom and dad doing?"

Angel gave a quick shake of her head. "I'm sorry, but you're not going to get off that easy, Daniel. I thought we were becoming friends, and you know practically everything there is to know about me. I even told you all about my disease." She leaned to put a hand on his arm again. "C'mon, Danny-Boy... You can share with me. Whatever it is, I won't judge you, and I promise not to tell anyone, either."

Daniel smirked. "Are you sure about that? I seem to remember you were a little judgmental last week when I told you about Sox."

Angel laughed and slapped his knee good naturedly. "I wasn't *judging* you; I was testing you, and maybe teasing you a little bit, too."

"Testing me. That's right. You did say something about that. Well, I hope I passed your stuffed-animal quiz."

"You'll find out soon enough," she said mysteriously. "But in the meantime, I noticed you looked happier this week. Did you try my suggestion of repeating, 'I am love, and I forgive and love myself'?"

Grateful for the change of subject, especially since he'd planned on telling Angel about how he'd felt better this past week, Daniel nodded. "Yep, I sure did. I admit it felt weird to talk to myself that way at first, but I got used to it after a few days." He glanced away. "During the last couple of years, I've been struggling with a lot of...negative thoughts. My shrink said I've been 'harboring hateful feelings', and I've been 'punishing myself with guilt'. I think he's probably right..."

"Whoa!" Angel reared back. "Wait a minute. Did you say a shrink? Have you been seeing a psychologist?"

"Actually, he's a psychiatrist, but I guess it's kind of the same thing, yeah." Daniel hesitated. He'd revealed a tiny part of his secret. How would this little kid handle the whole ugly truth? "Yes, as part of my rehabilitation, I've been ordered to seek professional help."

Angel shook her head. "Okay, Daniel, we need to back up. It's a good thing we're sitting in the dark right now because you don't want to see my confused face. The first time you came here, you slipped up and said something about being ordered to visit me, and now you say you're seeing a shrink as part of your 'rehabilitation'. How bad is it? Are you in big trouble? Why are you taking a break from technology? Why are you here, Daniel?"

Daniel squirmed in the chair and looked away. He hadn't been this nervous since he'd faced the judge the day of sentencing. Not only that, but Angel sounded as if she was an attorney, cross-examining a hostile witness. He leaped to his feet.

"I have to go, Angel. I have to go now."

"Okay," she said easily, surprising him, "but before you leave, can you please do me one more favor? Can you hit that switch on the wall, and turn my light on? I want to see you, and I want to show something to you."

What was she up to now, Daniel wondered, as he went to the wall near the door and found the light switch. Whatever it was, he'd probably be better off doing what she asked rather than trying to argue with her. At least she wasn't still grilling him with one question after another. He turned on the light and waited.

Her gaze went to his head, and her eyes grew wide. "Wow, Danny-Boy, your hat is red—the color of love! I can't believe you remembered. Or was it just an accident?" she asked him and winked.

Daniel smiled. "No, it wasn't an accident. I knew you'd be happy if I wore something red to visit with you tonight." He'd thrown on the hat at the last minute, right before he'd rushed out the door to catch the bus that evening, but he had chosen this particular one on purpose.

"Well, I'm really proud of you, and Red is proud of you, too!" She giggled, and her hands went to her blonde wig. "Did you notice my hair, Daniel?"

"You added an orange streak. It looks cool, but why did you pick orange, Angel?" She was beginning to look like Rainbow Brite, but Angel being Angel, she pulled off the look with finesse.

"I'll answer that question in a minute, but first, do me a favor, and turn the light back off." She nodded toward the switch.

Daniel frowned. He'd be leaving soon, and he hated to think of her sitting there, all alone in her dark hospital room. "Why do you want me to turn it off?" he asked her.

"Just do it, Daniel. I want to show you something. You came in here looking happy, and I sensed you were happy…that you were feeling a little more love than you usually do. Then something changed in you. You felt threatened, and your love switch turned off."

Daniel's frown deepened. "My love switch?"

"Don't feel bad, Danny-Boy; it happens to everyone. Our love switch gets turned on and off throughout the day. Our love becomes conditional, depending on our moods, feelings, interactions with others, and the memories we hold in our hearts."

"Angel, where do you come up with all this stuff?"

"Through one of my Google love searches, of course, and then I put it into practice in my own life. You see, Danny-Boy, I don't believe everything I read online, unless, of course, I can prove it. For instance, my online search for the two-headed cow resulted in four frustrating hours spent scanning pages of bizarre pictures. I never did find the two-headed cow, but I wasted four hours of my shortened life. That represents almost two percent of my remaining twenty-two hundred hours of life! That's why I'm keeping my love switch turned on, because life is too short not to love!"

Daniel stared at her for a moment and then shrugged. He walked back over to her bed and sank back down on the vinyl-covered chair. Obviously, he couldn't walk away now. She'd hooked him with her "life is too short not to love" statement, and now he had to stay and listen to her love-switch theory, or whatever it was. Not to mention, twenty-two hundred hours? A lump formed in his throat as he considered the fact that she was keeping track of how much time she had left. How could someone so sweet and innocent be contemplating her own mortality? The least he could do was give her his time and attention. Besides, if he left now, knowing Angel, she'd just pick up with the same story next week…

"Okay, Angel, I can stay for a little while longer, as long as the nurses don't kick me out."

"You're a brave man to risk facing the nurses' wrath." She gave him a lopsided smile, but her lips quivered, as if she were forcing herself to appear happy. "And you might think I'm a brave, little girl, but I was really scared and mad when I found out I had cancer. I was mad at the doctors for the diagnosis, mad at my mom and dad for raising a kid who ended up getting cancer, mad at my brother because he was healthy, mad at God for letting this happen, and I was mad at myself for getting sick. How could this happen to a sweet, seven-year-old kid? I felt sorry for myself, and I wanted to blame someone—everyone—anyone. I had dreams of growing up and becoming a teacher, but my dreams were dashed, and it felt like I was living in a nightmare. Some days, I would wake up and wish I could live in another kid's body and in another kid's life! It took a while for me to get over the 'poor me' feelings and to accept the illness that had invaded my body. The cancer wasn't my fault, and it wasn't anyone else's fault, either. I had to trade in my angry and hateful feelings for something that made me feel better, and I chose love!"

Daniel had sat in stunned silence as she'd confessed how angry and upset she'd been when she'd first gotten sick, and his respect for her only grew as he realized how horrible the last three months of her life must have been. And yet, she almost always seemed happy…and as she'd said, she'd overcome all that self-pity and hate. Instead, she'd chosen love. He shook his head. He felt humbled by her, this seven-year-old little girl who seemed to have a better handle on life—on living—than any adult he'd ever known.

"Wow," he said, struggling to find the words to tell her what he was thinking. "I can't imagine what you're going through, but I can understand those angry and hateful feelings you had. I'm proud of you for choosing love, and I want you to know you inspire me!"

She tilted her head but held his gaze. "Well, I think you should know, we have something in common because I saw a shrink, too. Ms. Allison helped me deal with my anger, and she encouraged me to practice forgiveness and acceptance. I followed her advice, and my curiosity led me to my online search for love." She paused and giggled. "Not the dating kind of love of course; I'm only seven, and my dad would have taken away my iPad if some kid showed up with a goofy smile and a dozen red roses. But what I've learned about love has been the greatest gift a kid with cancer could ask for, and now I want to share that gift with you!" She sat back against her pillows and gave him a serious, steady look. "Are you ready to receive it, Daniel?"

"Angel, you've already given me several gifts." In fact, she'd taught him more in the short time he'd known her than he'd learned from almost any other person in his life, except maybe his mom. Daniel decided then and there that he'd try to be honest with her—maybe even come totally clean sometime soon—and if she had more to show him about how to get rid of the heavy depression he'd been carrying around with him these last two-plus years, he'd damn well listen to her. He took a deep breath and spoke from his heart. "I'm grateful for our friendship, for your funny stories, and for your zest for life. I'm willing to listen and learn, but you'll have to be patient with me. I'm hurting pretty badly on the inside, and I guess that's why it shows on the outside."

Angel nodded. "Danny-Boy, I can feel your pain, but I also sense your desire to heal. Love heals, and love will help *you* heal."

Suddenly, Daniel felt drained—physically and emotionally wiped out. "I hope so, Angel, because I have a lot of healing to do," he told her, getting to his feet once again. "It's getting late, and I need to get going so you can get some rest. Don't stay up too long searching for love lessons or looking for a goofy-smiling kid with a dozen red roses, okay?"

"Ha-ha," she said. "Very funny. But I think I'll save my love for Red and for someone who brings me strawberry milkshakes." She winked. "I know you need to leave, but before you go, please promise me you'll continue repeating those words. Remember—*I am love, and I forgive and love myself.* Also, promise me you'll be aware of your love switch. If you notice your love is off, then please, make sure you turn it back on. You'll heal faster if your love switch is in the on position. If you need a love reminder, wear something red. I might just surprise you next week with some of my other favorite colors and the reasons I wear them." She waved him toward the door.

Daniel shook his head, too tired to argue or question her. "Good night, Angel."

"Oh, wait!"

He turned back toward the bed. "What's wrong?"

Angel pointed at the empty milkshake containers on her night table. "Please, take the evidence with you. If the nurses find those in here, they'll have a cow. Maybe even a two-headed cow!"

Daniel laughed as he scooped up the cups and stuck them inside his coat.

"And, Daniel, since I can't contact you online, remember Code Berries for next time, okay?" Her laugh turned into a yawn this time.

"Okay, but now I really do have to say good night. Sleep tight, and don't let the two-headed cows bite!"

Before Angel could come up with another request or goofy comment, Daniel slipped out of her room and headed down the hallway toward the steps. A quick glance at his watch told him visiting hours had ended thirty minutes earlier. As he entered the dimly lit, empty stairwell, he counted himself lucky that none of the nurses had seen him sneak out of Angel's room or spotted him with the two empty milkshake cups partially hidden under his jacket. He didn't want to cause any trouble for himself or for his little Angel. The judge's community service sentencing had caused enough of an uproar. They'd had to get special authorization from the hospice administration and approval from Angel's family. Before they'd even let him in the building, Daniel had to pass a screening in front of the entire staff. From what he'd heard, Angel's dad hadn't understood the judge's reasoning. He just wanted to protect his daughter, and he didn't give a damn about the rehabilitation of a twenty-one-year-old criminal. Surprisingly, Angel's mother supported the idea of Daniel socializing with her daughter, and she'd ultimately given her approval for the weekly visits. Maybe she'd known, somehow, that Daniel and Angel would connect like they had. Or maybe she just had a kind and loving heart, like her daughter.

Despite needing about twenty hours of sleep, Daniel arrived home feeling light on his feet and with a head full of swirling thoughts from his inspiring visit with Angel. She was slowly peeling away his protective cover, and like it or not, he was beginning to open up and allow her to see his vulnerable side. With her quirky kid's view of the world her innocence came through loud and clear. Could it really be that simple to heal his guilt and shame? Just by repeating, "I am love, and I forgive and love myself"? It seemed too easy, but Daniel *had* felt better since he'd started saying it.

"Besides," he said, addressing himself in the bathroom mirror as he put away his toothbrush, "it's not like I have anything to lose".

Before he climbed into bed that night, he decided he'd make a conscious effort this week to replace all the negative chatter in his head with more positive thoughts, including the love and forgiveness Luvffirmation.

He sighed. Hands crossed beneath his head, he stared up at the ceiling. He had a challenging week coming up. In addition to work, he had a meeting with his parole officer on Tuesday and dinner with his mother on Thursday night. He had finally accepted her invitation to come over for an old-fashioned, home-cooked meal, but she would probably ask more questions than his parole officer.

That was one of his biggest issues these days; everyone he knew seemed as if they were passing judgment on him—heck, even strangers seemed to give him the suspicious eye. Maybe he gave off some kind of "I'm guilty" vibe, and if he could learn to forgive himself, then maybe others would forgive him, too. His thoughts kept drifting back to Angel's words, and deep down inside, he knew she was right. She spoke directly to his heart, and being around her made him feel less like a guilty, ex-convict every day. The first three visits with her had been less frightening and a lot more enlightening than he had ever expected.

Daniel rolled onto his side, hugged his pillow, closed his eyes, and smiled. He was actually looking forward to the remaining five weeks of his community service visits with his little Angel.

****

That Tuesday, Daniel's meeting with his parole officer went pretty much as he'd expected—professional but basically uneventful. The officer asked the standard questions, and Daniel provided the disciplined answers. He'd learned the hard way not to divulge too much information. He provided short but respectful responses so the officer could tick off the appropriate boxes on the answer form. These meetings, which he had every other week, had become a bit of a chess game. If Daniel tried to make an offensive move, the officer would have to counter with a defensive list of additional questions. The legal system seemed to expect him to play the rehabilitation game according to their rules, timelines, and expectations. Daniel didn't dare offer any information regarding his insightful lessons from his visits with Angel. No sense in opening up a potential can of worms! Instead, he told them what they wanted to hear. He said the weekly visits at the hospice were helping him adjust back into society. He always ended the session by thanking the parole officer for his time and attention. If only the PO knew what the sick kid was teaching Daniel. Maybe the savvy, old judge had known Daniel would get schooled in life by a spunky kid who, despite her terminal illness, was full of love and life!

****

Mothers always know best, and in Daniel's eyes, his mom was one of the smartest, kindest women on the planet. While he'd been the one who'd gone to prison and spent two years behind bars, his mother had suffered nearly as much as he had. Every time she'd come to see him on visiting days, he could sense how badly she'd been wounded by what he'd done, but she never said anything to him about it…never blamed him or told him how stupid he'd been. Instead, she'd spent all her time telling him everything would be okay and encouraging him when he'd been particularly down.

Once he'd been released from jail, she'd wanted him to come to stay with her for a while until he got back on his feet. Of course, he'd refused. She had this way of knowing when he was down or depressed, and then she'd worry or get upset, and the last thing he wanted to do was cause her more pain. And since he hadn't exactly been in a great mood lately, for the most part, he'd avoided her these last months. All she'd need to do is take one look at his face to know he wasn't happy, and then she wouldn't be happy, and 'round and 'round it would go, a messed-up circle of guilt and remorse…

This week, however, when she'd phoned to invite him to dinner—as she did every week—instead of allowing his answering machine to take the call, he'd picked up the phone and told her he'd love to come by.

The air brakes squealed as the city bus came to a stop, three blocks away from his mother's house. As Daniel disembarked, he smiled, recalling her reaction when he'd told her that yes, he'd come for dinner that Thursday. At first, he'd heard nothing but dead silence, and for a moment, he'd thought maybe the call had gotten disconnected somehow. But in the next instant, she'd let out a joyous shout that had him holding the receiver away from his ear a little bit. Then she'd begun rattling off the menu—fried chicken, mashed potatoes, and a green-bean casserole, which she knew was one of his favorites—speaking so excitedly, Daniel had to struggle to take it all in.

"I love you, son," she'd told him, just before they'd hung up. "And I can't wait to see you."

Daniel had a bounce to his step as he strode along the sidewalk toward home. *Home...* He hadn't been back there since...before, and he had to admit, he was looking forward to seeing the old place again, couldn't wait to sit with his mom at her tiny, Formica-topped kitchen table and listen to her gossip about work and her friends over hot cups of freshly brewed coffee.

"Daniel!"

The door swung open the moment he reached the front stoop, almost as if his mom had been watching for him. Chances were good she probably had been.

"Hi, Mom." He gave her a small smile.

"Well, don't just stand there; come on in." She grabbed his hand and pulled him inside.

The mouthwatering aroma of fried chicken greeted him the moment he entered the front foyer.

"Oh, man, that smells delicious!" He preceded her into the kitchen, following his nose, and began lifting the lids off pots and covered serving dishes. "There's a lot more here than just fried chicken, mashed potatoes, and green-bean casserole." In fact, she'd cooked enough food to feed a small army.

"Well, I figured there was no tellin' what you've been eating lately, and the last time I saw you—which was months ago, I might add—you were far too skinny." She gave him a onceover. "You're still too skinny. Now, sit yourself down, and let me get this meal on the table."

"Let me help—."

"Sit down!" She pointed at the table against the wall beneath the window.

Daniel smiled. "Yes, ma'am."

He watched and waited as patiently as his growling stomach would allow, while she brought bowl after bowl after platter over and set them on the table. When she finally took her seat across from him, he placed his napkin on his lap like she'd taught him to do when he was small and quickly bowed his head to say grace.

"Thank you, Lord, for this food we are about to receive, and bless and help those less fortunate. Amen."

"Amen." His mother passed him the platter of chicken. "So, talk to me, boy. Tell me how you're liking that job of yours, and what about the community service? How's that working out for you?"

As Daniel continued piling food on his plate, he told his mom about his position at the call center, doing his best to make it sound better than it was. After all, why complain about a job he only looked at as temporary—a means to an end—regardless of how boring and repetitive he found it?

His mom listened carefully, nodding now and then, and when he paused, she reached across the table and put her hand on his.

"And what about the volunteer thing at the hospice?" she asked him. "Are you okay? It's not making you more depressed than you already were, is it?"

Daniel turned his hand, palm up, so he could grasp his mom's hand and give it a squeeze. "It's actually really great," he told her. "I mean, *really* great. The kid I go see every Friday night—her name's Angel—is about as cute as a seven-year-old little girl can be, and she's super smart, Mom." He paused, set down his fork, and leaned back in his chair. "It's crazy, really. If someone would have told me three weeks ago that a precocious little angel would have more to teach me about life than any three philosophers combined, I would have laughed. But she has, Ma…" He nodded to emphasize his words. "She really has."

His mother tipped her head, as if considering what he'd just told her. "She's seven years old, you say? That's very young. I'm assuming she's— I mean, she has to be—" She broke off, her cheeks turning red.

"Dying. Yeah, she is." Daniel said the words, but he couldn't bring himself to actually confront the truth in them. Not now. Maybe not ever. He felt as if he and Angel still had many, many hours of conversation ahead of them, and he simply could not imagine going into her room and not seeing her there. He shook his head. "But she doesn't act like it. At least, not when I'm there. She's a little tease, likes to joke around and have fun. And she loves the color red and strawberry milkshakes."

He grinned. His mom probably thought he sounded silly, chattering on about a seven-year-old kid, but Daniel didn't care. Angel made him happy; more importantly, she'd begun to make him look at life and at himself differently. Suddenly, it became very important to him that he make his mother understand.

"Like I told you, she's really smart. I'm guessing since she's sick, she spends a lot of time reading about all kinds of stuff online. And she's got these ideas about love—she says everyone is worthy of love, and it's important for people to start by loving themselves." He went on to tell her briefly about what Angel called Luvffirmations and how she had reminded him to turn on his "love switch."

His mother got up from the table and went to start a pot of coffee. They'd finished their dinner while they'd talked, so Daniel cleared away their dirty plates and began setting the leftovers on the counter. He'd help his mom put them into storage containers later, after they'd rested their stomachs a while.

The coffee finished brewing, and his mom poured them each a mug, adding a lot of cream and just a little sugar to both. They'd always taken their coffee the same way—probably because he'd learned to drink the stuff in the first place by copying her. She grabbed a pie, two dessert plates, and a couple forks and set them on the end of the table. Then she got their coffee and came back to sit down again. She took a sip, set the mug on the table, and wrapped both hands around it, the way Daniel always did when his fingers were cold.

"She sounds delightful and wise beyond her years," his mother finally said in response to the things he'd told her about Angel. "And if that little girl has anything at all to do with the change I can see in your eyes and hear in your voice, then I love her already."

Daniel thought about that a moment. Had he really changed all that much since starting his visits with Angel? He considered the past week, how he'd felt more at ease with his coworkers, how he'd started to wake up in the morning feeling differently about the upcoming day. Maybe he still didn't look forward to riding the bus to a dead-end, mindless job, but at least he didn't walk around feeling as if his life was over, or filled with so much guilt or anger, his shoulders actually ached from the weight of those awful emotions.

"Yeah." He nodded. "I guess I have changed. A little. And I—*we*—definitely have Angel to thank for that."

"Well, I knew that judge was no dummy. You think maybe he set this up—put you two together—I mean you and her specifically—knowing what would come of it?"

Daniel shrugged. "Maybe. I know you were all for the idea when he handed down his sentence."

"Well, that part of it, at least. I still don't think you should have served any prison time, and—"

"Mom." Daniel held up a hand to stop the coming tirade. One he'd heard several times before. "What's done is done, and all that stuff is in the past."

The look on his mom's face appeared to reflect the shock he felt over what he'd just said. Did he really believe that? Were all those things in the past? No... Absolutely not! Well, some of it. The time he'd spent behind bars, definitely. But the other stuff? The thing he'd done that had caused a judge to send him away for two years, to give him eight weeks of community service, and to forbid him from having anything at all to do with the Internet or cellphones? No... all those things were still a part of his everyday life, still fresh in his mind, still sickened him when he allowed himself to dwell on them too much, examine them too closely.

"Mom, I—"

"No need to explain. I know what you mean, Daniel. There are some things we're not meant to forget. But that doesn't mean we have to allow them to haunt us, to stunt our growth or prevent us from loving or believing we're worthy of love." She nodded toward the apple pie. "That's fresh baked just this morning. Would you like a slice?"

"Oh, God, no!" Daniel sat back, patted his over-extended belly, and laughed. "If I eat another bite, I think I'll explode." He took a last swallow of his coffee and got to his feet. "In fact, I'm going to put this food away, and then I'm going to get on home. I have work in the morning and then another visit with my little angel."

"Your 'little angel', huh?" His mother teased him.

Daniel's cheeks grew red and he ducked his head. "Yeah, I guess I've kind of come to think of her as a little sister or something. She's sweet."

His mom got up and joined him at the counter. She put a hand on his shoulder.

"Coming to care for someone is nothing to be ashamed of, Daniel. And as for helping me put away all this food, you'll do no such thing; I've got this. You"—she reached inside the refrigerator and pulled out a grocery store bag filled with plastic food storage containers—"take this. I put together some things for you to take home with you. There's a little bit of everything we had tonight, plus, I made a cobbler out of the apples I had left over after I made the pie. That's in there, too."

A wave of love and admiration for his kind, generous, thoughtful mother washed over him, and Daniel set the plastic bag on the counter so he could wrap her in a hug.

"You're something else, you know that?" he asked, his voice thick. He released her and stepped back, wiping at the tears that threatened to spill over. "I won't be too skinny for long if you keep feeding me like that."

"I love you, Daniel." She handed him back the bag. "Now go on home, and get some rest. I'll give you a call on Sunday, and maybe we can do this again next Thursday?"

"Absolutely!"

She walked him to the door and stood on the threshold, watching him as he went down the walkway and out the little gate onto the main sidewalk that ran along the street. He closed the gate behind him, looked back at his mom, and waved good-bye. He headed back toward the bus stop, swinging his sack of goodies and whistling, his heart feeling lighter than it had in a very, very long time… What might it be like to live his life in such a way that he knew he was making his mother proud? Sure, she loved him. She had to; she was his mother. But could he get his act together, do something…better? Something that would make her think highly of him and brag about him to her friends.

His mother was the only person in his life he could confide in these days, and even though he was grateful for her unconditional love and support, he'd spent a lot of time pushing her away or avoiding her lately. As he boarded the bus back home, he vowed to change that situation—starting now.

WEEK 4

Friday evening arrived, and an outside observer would have thought Daniel was headed to see his favorite band play or to meet a famous movie star. He'd been grinning like a fool ever since he'd stopped at the restaurant a block down the road from the hospice, and when he entered the back stairwell, he took the steps two at a time.

He arrived on the third floor out of breath and paused a moment to gingerly stuff the milkshakes inside his partially zipped jacket, one in each side, where he could kind of hold them against his torso with his arms so they wouldn't tip over. As he strode down the hallway toward Angel's room, a nurse coming from the opposite direction gave him a questioning look as she passed, but luckily, she didn't stop him.

"Angel, hey, kid?" He stepped inside her room and looked around.

The smile slipped from his face at the sight of her empty bed. Where had she gone? Had they taken her to another part of the building for some kind of treatments? Or maybe she was down the other end of the hallway, in the kids' common area the hospice administrator had shown him when he'd originally been interviewed by the staff. The sick children sometimes got together to watch television, play games, or hold group activities in the large room. Maybe Angel had decided to join them tonight? As Daniel turned to leave to see if he could find her, a noise from the adjoining bathroom brought him to a halt.

"Angel?"

He went to stand outside the closed bathroom door. "Angel? You okay?"

The unmistakable sound of someone getting sick turned Daniel's excitement to concern, and concern quickly turned to worry and downright fear, as those awful retching sounds continued.

He turned away from the door, intending to sound the nurses' call alarm and ask someone to come and help.

"Daniel, is that you?" Angel asked from inside the bathroom, her voice shaky and weak. "I'm okay, and I'll be out in just a minute. Please, wait for me."

"Are you sure?" he asked her. "I can go get one of the nurses—"

"No!" Her response came swift and strong. "No. I'll be right out."

Daniel sighed and leaned his shoulder against the wall outside the bathroom door to wait. He heard the toilet flush several times followed by the sound of water running in the sink. A moment later, Angel came out, moving slowly, her face deathly pale. The sight shocked him so badly, for an instant, he couldn't think of anything to say.

"Wait right there," he told her.

He turned around and went over to her little nightstand, where he unloaded the milkshakes, removing them from their hiding spot inside his jacket and placing them on the table. He then went back to where Angel stood, one hand braced on the doorjamb, as if she needed the support to keep from falling over. Daniel's stomach clenched, and he shook his head.

"C'mere."

He put an arm around her tiny shoulders and helped her shuffle over to her bed.

"You sure you're all right," he asked her. The last thing he wanted to do was help her up into bed, just to have her start getting sick again.

She looked up at him and nodded. Her forlorn expression tugged at his heart, and he pulled her in for a big but gentle hug.

"Ew, Daniel, I must stink like puke. You don't have to touch me."

She tried to pull away, but he wasn't having it. In fact, he hugged her more tightly, despite the sick odor that clung to her hair and her vomit-stained gown.

"I'm so sorry you're sick, Angel," he whispered, holding her close. "Is there anything I can do for you?"

She looked up at him, a hint of her angelic nature shining through. "Actually, there is." She wiggled free, climbed from the bed, and went back into the bathroom, returning a moment later with what looked like a can of air freshener. She held it out to him. "Spray me."

"What?" He took a step back, hands up, refusing to take the can. "No...I can't. What is that, Angel?"

"It's a lemon air freshener. They keep a can in all of our bathrooms. You know, sometimes sick kids can make a room pretty smelly. You have to spray me, Daniel. I know I stink, and I want to smell like fresh lemons." She giggled and turned her head so he could see the side. "Plus, the lemon smell will match my pretty yellow streak that I added to my hair."

"Yeah, but those air fresheners are full of toxic chemicals, and they are not supposed to be used on people, let alone on a sick kid." Had she gotten this idea off the Internet, too? If so, it wasn't nearly as good as some of the other stuff she'd found online.

"Oh, no! Danny-Boy, do you think it could cause cancer or make my hair fall out?" she asked, tongue in cheek. Her eyes sparkled, a contrast to her pasty-white complexion.

"Oh, you're a funny sick kid tonight, aren't you?" he asked her, shaking his head over what he was about to do. "Okay, we'll do things your way. I guess it wouldn't hurt to turn you into a fresh lemon. Besides, strawberries and lemons smell great together."

Angel bounced up and down. "Code Berries?" She looked over toward her nightstand. "Is that what you put on my table?"

He nodded. The tops of the milkshake cups were barely visible in between all the different stuffed animals and cards she had sitting there. "Yep. I remembered."

"Danny-Boy, you're my hero!" She held out the can again. "Now spray me down so I can get back into bed, and you and I can have our treat!"

"Okay." He took the air freshener. "But cover your eyes. I'm pretty sure this stuff would burn."

As Daniel sprayed, Angel covered her face with her hands and slowly turned all the way around until she faced him again.

"There," he said, putting the lid back onto the can. "All done. You climb up into bed, and I'll put this back in your bathroom."

When he opened the bathroom door, the smell of puke hit him in the face. *Ugh!* He took the lid off the can again and sprayed a bunch of the air freshener all over the little room. For good measure, he turned on the exhaust fan before shutting off the light and closing the door again.

How the doctors and nurses dealt with all these sick little kids, Daniel would never know. Not only did they have to handle things like vomiting and—other bodily functions—they had to watch some of them… maybe *most* of them get sicker and sicker until eventually, the kids died. He couldn't imagine how they must feel. *I mean, they gotta become attached to the these kids. At least some of them,* he thought. How could they do their jobs every day, knowing the people they were caring for—the people they'd come to care *about*—would eventually die?

Daniel turned to go join Angel for their evening snack and froze in his tracks, his mind racing. Unless a miracle happened, *Angel* would die in just a few weeks. The thought made his stomach churn and his eyes burn. But Angel was sitting on the bed, grinning at him, no doubt waiting as patiently as a seven-year-old, little girl could wait for him to hand over her strawberry milkshake. Not wanting to let her down—or burden her with his sadness— Daniel shoved the morose thoughts away and forced a smile.

"Your arms broken?" he asked her, nodding toward her sidetable. "Grab those shakes for us, would you?"

He went to the chair he always used and took a seat, propping his feet up on the bedrails that ran underneath her mattress.

Angel reached over, carefully picked up his shake, and handed it to him. She then grabbed hers and settled back onto the pile of pillows stacked behind her. She took a long draw on the straw, closed her eyes, and moaned.

"Oh, my goodness! This milkshake is making my tummy feel ever so much better!" she told him.

Daniel nodded. "I'm happy to hear that, Angel, but please…sip slowly. You don't want to lose all that delicious shake by making yourself sick again." He frowned. "It won't make you sick, will it? I mean, I know the pizza didn't go over so well. The last thing I want is to make you feel any worse than you already do."

"I don't think anything could make me feel any worse than I already did a little bit ago," she told him. "And besides, a strawberry milkshake has milk in it, right? They give us milk here all the time. I'm sure I'll be fine, and like I said, it's making me feel much, much better, so don't worry about it."

For a few moments, neither of them spoke, as they both sat quietly, enjoying their treat.

But as Angel neared the bottom of her cup and began making slurping sounds, she paused and looked up at him. "This milkshake brought me back to life," she said, "but there's something else that makes me feel more alive, and I think it's important for me to share this with you because you might need some life-saving energy someday."

"If I do, can't I just buy another strawberry milkshake?" he teased her.

Angel frowned, her expression turning serious. "Daniel…"

He sighed. Her cute, childlike demeanor had disappeared, replaced by the more adult persona she tended to use when she wanted to discuss something important with him. Her ability to converse like a college professor still amazed him.

"Okay," he told her, "I'm listening. What is this life-saving advice you have for me?"

"Well, no offense, Danny-Boy, but you look like you could use some help. Although I'm only seven, I didn't start living or loving until I found out I only had six months left. I started living when I realized I loved life and everyone in my life. It might be hard to understand, but I feel like I've lived a lifetime in the last several weeks. I appreciate everything, everyone, and every moment—especially the strawberry-milkshake-slurping moments!" She paused to grin at him, giving him a glimpse of her impish-little-girl side. "Does that make sense, Daniel? I just wish you could feel what I feel. Not the sick feelings or the way I feel sometimes when I look in the mirror and see my bald head, but the amazing-appreciation-for-life feelings. I love life, and I love you, too, Danny-Boy! I just wish I could convince others how precious life is. Maybe then, people would have fewer worries, fears, shame, anger, jealousy, and all those other negative feelings and emotions."

Daniel considered her words. She had a point; if everyone in the world could learn to appreciate life's littlest gifts and to love one another, planet Earth would be a much nicer place. "I admit I don't know how you feel, but I'm trying to be more grateful and loving these days. It's not that easy—especially when life sucks, and my life has really sucked during the last few years. I wish I could go back and change things, but I can't, and I feel stuck…unable to get rid of all these feelings of shame and regret."

"I'm not saying it's easy, but it's important—*super* important—to learn to love yourself, to love your life, and to love others, too! There are times I wish I could magically remove the cancer, grow up as a normal kid, go to school, become a teacher, get married, and even have kids of my own, but that life is not in the cards for me. It's not my destiny or my fate. My fate is to live out the remaining months with as much love as I can muster. Can you feel how much I love you?" she asked him.

"Yes." Every time she looked at him, he could see her love for him reflected in her gaze.

"Do you love me, Danny-Boy?" she asked, batting her eyelashes.

"Yes, Angel, I do. Even though we've only known each other a very short time, I've grown to love you. You're one of the sweetest kids I've ever met." He paused, then added, "Not that I've met a lot of kids…"

"Daniel!" She leaned forward and tapped him on his knee.

"Just kidding. Just kidding!"

She nodded. "I know you are, but like I said, this is important. The fact that you love *me* proves you're capable of loving others. Now, all you have to do is work on embracing unconditional self-love. Do you think you'll be able to master that, Danny-Boy?"

He heaved a heavy sigh, wondering if he'd ever be able to live up to other people's standards—Angel's, his mother's, the judge's…even society's, in general. He wanted to…he really did. "I'm trying, Angel, and I've been repeating the Luvffirmation you shared with me, and I actually think it's helping. I didn't get to tell you yet, but I went for dinner at my mom's last night, and we had a really nice visit." He looked down at his milkshake. "I've kind of been avoiding her lately because I've been afraid to open up to her—plus, *she* gets upset when she sees *me* upset, so I've just been staying away. But we had a really good visit last night, and I told her about you and your views on life and love. I should bring her to meet you someday. I think you'd really like her, and I know she'd love you." He paused and smiled. "She'd especially love all those colorful streaks in your hair."

"I can tell you really love her," Angel said.

"Yeah, I do, and I appreciate everything she's done for me. She's been my rock when I felt weak, and she never stopped caring about me… even when I didn't care for myself very much. I broke her heart, I think, and even though she says she's forgiven me, I still feel like I need to do something—become a better person or something—to make up for all the pain I've caused."

"A mother's love for a child is like no other, and I'm certain she's proud of you now, no matter what happened in your past." She looked away, and her eyes filled with tears. "Sometimes, I feel sad when I think how my mom will feel when I'm gone. I've heard her cry several times, and I just hope and pray she can accept my fate. I overheard her say that a mother should never have to bury her child."

Daniel closed his eyes as a wave of guilt and pain hit him like a physical punch in the gut. He felt as if he was drowning in a sea of sorrow.

"I need to—" Daniel started to rise. He had to get out of there before he broke down completely.

"Daniel, what's wrong?" Angel asked. "Please, sit back down and listen to me for a minute. This is so important, and you can't keep running. Haven't you ever heard the saying, 'Wherever you go, there you are'? You can't run from yourself, Daniel." She paused and gave him a scrutinizing stare. "I can tell just by looking at you that your love light is completely off, and you're stuck in a dark place right now. You can't go through life without ever sharing your burdens, or you'll be crushed under their weight." She leaned forward and put a hand on his knee. "I'm here for you, and I am not going to let you shrug me off this time. You've been running away from whatever has been torturing you, and maybe it's time to face your demons. Daniel, I told you before—I'm not going to judge you or criticize you or look down on you in any way. I want to help you, and I believe in synchronicities." She paused and smiled. "Big word for a little girl, huh? But I can't think of one that does a better job describing how I feel. We've come together for a reason, and I think that reason has something to do with you being so sad. Please, have faith, and trust that maybe I can shed some light on your dark feelings." She sat back and grinned. "You know I have three powers, and they all begin with the letter I: insight, intuition, and my iPad—so try to see me as your Love Angel. You have nothing to lose and possibly a lot to gain. Besides, I feel obligated to give you something in return for those delicious, strawberry milkshakes!"

"Okay…" Daniel leaned back, closed his eyes, and laced his hands behind his head, face to the ceiling. "You're wearing me down, but I'm warning you; you're not going to be very happy with what I'm about to tell you. In fact, you're going to be really disappointed, and you probably won't want to see me ever again." Once he shared his secret, he imagined this would be the last time he'd get to visit with her.

"Let me be the judge of that, Daniel. In case you haven't noticed, I'm a very strong little girl, *and* I know how to forgive."

That was an understatement. Angel might be the strongest *person* he knew, let alone little girl. She was strong and smart and kind—just as he'd told his mother. But he had a feeling she'd never had a friend tell her anything like what he was about to tell her.

Still, he figured she had a right to know the truth about what kind of person she was associating with—after all, she'd just told him she loved him. And these visits with her had made such a huge difference in his life. Although he hadn't come there because he wanted to at first, he'd grown to look forward to Friday evenings, and he'd never regret the connection he'd made with his little Angel.

Daniel straightened up, opened his eyes, and held Angel's curious gaze. If this was going to be his last visit with her, then he was going to be open and honest with her, regardless of how much pain he might cause.

He cleared his throat. "First of all, kiddo, you have to know it wasn't my choice to volunteer at the hospice or to visit you. I was sentenced by a judge to do community service work, and this is where they sent me."

Angel laughed. "Well, *kiddo*, I didn't pick *you*, either; in fact, I was surprised when you showed up in my room. Being sentenced to do community service work at a hospice doesn't seem too severe of a punishment. Whatever you did, it couldn't be all that bad."

"You don't understand… That was only part of my punishment. I also served two years in a medium-security prison. It was the scariest two years of my life, but I'm not complaining because I deserved every minute of my sentence. In fact, I deserve worse!"

Angel sat up in her bed. She wasn't laughing now, and, apparently, Daniel had gotten her full attention. She had a scared look on her face, and when he shifted closer, intending to tell her the rest of it, she scooted away a little bit. Daniel wished he could rewind time, take it all back, and erase that frightened gleam in her eyes, but it was too late. He'd come this far—he had no choice but to trudge on.

"Angel, look, I *did* do something terrible, but I'm *not* some dangerous ex-con, and you have nothing to be afraid of. It was an accident. Even though I was held criminally responsible, I didn't do it on purpose."

"Oh, my God, Daniel, what happened?" She leaned toward him again. Either she'd decided he wasn't a danger, or her curiosity had overridden her fear.

Daniel sat silently for a moment, staring off into space, allowing his thoughts to drift back to that day a little over two years ago. A day he hadn't allowed himself to fully recall in a very long time. He sucked in his breath then sighed. "It was the end of the school year, and I was at a friend's barbecue. It was the middle of the afternoon, and I'd had a couple of beers. My girlfriend sent me a text and asked if I could pick her up after work and bring her back to the barbecue. I felt I was okay to drive, so I left my friend's place and went to pick her up. She sent me a text while I was driving, and I only looked down for a minute, but that was all it took. I didn't mean to; I swear I didn't mean to."

Daniel's thoughts careened back to the scene that had met his eyes when he'd looked back up and out through the windshield. God, how he hated remembering these things, never mind talking about them. Daniel swallowed back a sob and wondered if he'd be able to speak past the lump that had formed in his throat.

"Hey," Angel whispered and patted the mattress beside her. "Come here." She'd scooted even closer to him, but there was still plenty of room for him to join her on the bed.

Daniel got to his feet then slumped down beside her, and then he poured out the entire, tragic, emotional story, while tears of regret poured down his cheeks.

"I was driving the speed limit, but I wasn't paying attention. I looked up at the scene in front of me, and I froze. I saw her in the crosswalk, but it was too late. I slammed on the brakes as hard as I could, but my car didn't stop in time. The next thing I knew, I heard a sickening sound as her little body slammed into my windshield." His voice broke on a sob, but he forced himself to go on. Angel deserved to know the whole, ugly truth. "I saw the little girl's blood-stained face through the shattered windshield, and I kn-knew she was d-d-dead. I couldn't move. I felt paralyzed. F-frozen with fear. Someone reached in and dragged me out of the car, and then

I was swarmed by all these angry people, all of them threatening me and saying they smelled alcohol on my breath and that they'd seen the buzzing cellphone on the front seat.

"One lady kept asking me, 'How could you do such a thing? How could you do something so horrible?' and another woman just kept screaming, 'You killed her, you killed her', over and over.

"And another lady—I found out later it was the little girl's mother—came racing over from the house across the street. She was screaming and sobbing, and I guess she watched the whole thing happen from her front porch. The lady fell on her knees beside her daughter's lifeless body, and when she looked up, she stared right at me, and I could read the agony in her eyes…"

Daniel hung his head and sobbed softly for a few moments, as he recalled the horror he'd felt over what he'd done. Thankfully, there wasn't much else to tell.

"I heard sirens, and then I must have blacked out," he whispered, "because the next thing I remember, I woke up in a hospital bed. My mother was sitting in a chair beside me, and there was a police officer standing at the door staring at me like I was some kind of three-headed monster."

"Oh, my God, Daniel, that's terrible! I'm so sorry. I can't imagine what you went through."

He looked at her and frowned. "What I went through? I mean, yeah, it sucked…was the worst thing I ever experienced, but I don't want you to feel sorry for me. I took a life. I killed an innocent, little girl. She was about your age, Angel, and I stole her from her mother and her family. I changed their lives forever. I'm still here, but she's gone, and she's never coming back. If you want to feel sorry for someone, feel sorry for her family and all the other innocent people whose lives I destroyed."

"You're right, Daniel, they do deserve our deepest sympathies, thoughts, and prayers." She paused to grab his hand and squeeze it. "*But so do you!* It was an *accident*, and although you made some bad choices, you didn't do it on purpose. You've served your time, and now you're doing your community service, and that's all part of the formal punishment. But you're still punishing yourself, and that self-imposed punishment will never go away unless you can forgive yourself."

"You have no idea how hard it is to do that," he told her. "For months afterward, I relived that horrible accident over and over again, and I hated myself. I wasn't legally drunk, but if I hadn't had a couple of beers, my reaction time would have been quicker. If I hadn't looked down at my phone, I would have seen that little girl in the crosswalk. All of these *ifs* haunt me every day. The sound of that little girl's mother screaming in emotional pain still keeps me awake at night, and sometimes, when I close my eyes"—Daniel shuddered—"I can see the little girl's lifeless eyes staring back at me through the shattered windshield."

Daniel had started breathing hard and feared he might hyperventilate. Talking about all these horrible memories had to be the most difficult thing he'd ever done.

"Shh. Hey, Danny-Boy, calm down. Calm down." Angel moved closer and patted his back. "It's going to be okay. Right now, you're trapped in a reoccurring nightmare. Thank goodness, you're getting professional help, and thank God you came into my life."

Daniel snorted. "Are you serious? I'm a mess!" He scoffed at her last statement. "After what I just told you, how could you possibly be *happy* to know me?"

"Do you believe everything—and I mean everything—happens for a reason? Most people struggle with this concept, especially when *everything* includes tragedies, accidents, or even serious crimes. There's always a bigger picture at play, but sometimes, it's hard to understand the reasons why or how we fit into the big picture. I saw a news clip the other night of a killer storm that swept through a small, Midwest town. On one side of the main street, hardly any buildings or homes were affected, but the other side of the street had been demolished. I'm talkin' complete devastation, and a lot of innocent people died. Why do you suppose that happened? I mean, why did that tornado only strike one side of the town? I'm sure the storm-shocked residents were asking the same thing, don't you think?"

Daniel nodded. He'd heard about similar incidents and had always wondered why some people were spared while others weren't. He'd always just chalked it up to fate or chance.

"But think about this… Maybe we're not supposed to ask why," she told him. "Maybe we're supposed to just accept—you know that old saying: 'it is what it is'. If we can learn to accept our fate and other people's fate, then maybe we can accept that everything happens for a reason. This would allow us to become more forgiving. Since forgiveness leads to the flow of unconditional love, we would be able to shed the negative emotions, like guilt, anger, and fear, and replace them with the power of unconditional love. Imagine what our world would be like if more and more people started to show unconditional love. We could light up the world with love, Danny-Boy!

"Angel, sometimes, I feel like I am talking to a highly educated scholar or a wise, old philosopher, and not a seven-year-old kid." He laughed and then shrugged. "What you're saying makes sense, but life isn't that simple. The accident was my fault, and I'm responsible for taking a little kid's life. I know I can't change what happened, but I can't forget about it, either!"

Angel sighed. "Daniel, no one expects you to forget, but for your own peace of mind, you need to forgive yourself." She spoke in a patient tone, as if their roles were reversed, and he was the little kid. "You've already started the healing process, and if you continue repeating the Forgiveness Luvffirmation and take steps to turn your love switch on, you will be able to love yourself unconditionally and love others unconditionally, too! And once that happens, you'll feel amazing; it's a real…trip! How does that sound, Danny-Boy? Are you ready to walk with me on this healing love journey?"

Daniel laughed. She had an unusal way of phrasing things, but she also seemed to make a lot of sense most of the time. At this point, all he knew for certain was that he'd felt better—a lot better—since he'd started visiting this kid and taking her advice to heart. "Angel, I knew after our first visit that I was meant to be here. I appreciate everything you've taught me already, so yeah, I think I'm willing to join you on this 'healing love journey', as you call it." He laughed again as a thought occurred to him. "Hey! Maybe your dream of becoming a teacher is coming true?"

She gave him a small smile. "Well, that would be a great thing to knock off my bucket list, Danny-Boy, because becoming a teacher is going to be a lot easier than getting married and having kids of my own! Mind you, I could always adopt. What do you think, Daniel, would I make a good mother?"

Her question sent a wave of sadness through him. Angel would never get to find out. "I'm sure you would make a great mother, Angel," he said softly. And then in an attempt to lighten the mood a little, he added, "But you would probably spoil your kids rotten feeding them pizza and strawberry milkshakes!"

Just as he'd hoped, Angel responded with a giggle.

"Oh, now wouldn't that be fun?" She giggled again. "Not that I'd want a bunch of spoiled kid's, but imagine all the delicious pizza and strawberry milkshake parties! Yum, yum, yum!"

"Yeah, but remember," he told her seriously, "what goes in a kid's sensitive tummy can come out just as fast!"

"Now who's sounding like the wise one—or maybe you're just being a smart-ass! Thanks for puking that out, I mean, pointing that out." She gave a dramatic sigh. "I guess I'll have to stick with the teacher role. Besides, teachers love getting treats from their students, and *good* students know to bring treats for their teachers!" She paused and glanced up at him. "Do I have to spell that out for you, Danny-Boy?"

"I know; I know… Code Berries." He wrapped an arm around her tiny shoulders and gave her a gentle squeeze. "I also know how to treat my favorite teacher."

She grinned then, no doubt already thinking about next Friday's milkshake. "I knew I could count on you. So, let's conclude today's lessons because your teacher is getting tired. I need to get cleaned up and go to bed."

Daniel nodded. He gave her one more brief hug then got to his feet. "I agree. I'm emotionally exhausted, so I can only imagine how you must be feeling right now. I hope your stomach doesn't give you any more trouble." He adjusted the sleeves on his jacket. "Oh, yeah! There was something I wanted to show you." He pushed his left sleeve up a little to reveal a bright-red rubber wristband. "This was a gift from my mom. She tried to give it to me when I first went to prison, but in there, they've got all kinds of rules about what you can and can't have, and I guess this wasn't on the list…" He shrugged. "Anyway, she kept it for me and gave it to me the day I got out." He held out his arm so Angel could get a good look. "See? It's engraved with the word love, and she wanted me to wear it as a reminder that she loved me."

"Aw, that's really sweet!" She touched the rubber band with her fingertips. "But it's probably just as well they didn't allow you to wear that in prison. I imagine that would have been like you wearing a large sign that read: boyfriend for hire." She giggled, hand to her mouth.

"Angel! What would a seven-year-old little girl know about such a thing?" he asked, only half-faking his shock over what she'd just said.

"Well, don't tell anyone, but I streamed a couple of episodes of that show *Orange is the New Black*, so I got a glimpse of prison life. Anyways, I am really glad you showed me your red love wristband, and I hope your fellow prisoners treated you with respect. I was going to say, 'with love and respect', but I guess you have to be careful about turning your love switch on in those dark, lonely cells. But now that you're out, I hope you continue wearing your red love band as a reminder of the power of love. I'm curious, though; which do you think is worse, hospital food or prison food?"

"Having tasted both at different times in my life, I'd have to say hospital food tastes a heck of a lot better." He shook a finger at her. "And if you keep getting into trouble, you might get the opportunity to find out for yourself!"

"Hey, I'm just a poor, little sick kid, remember? Sentencing me to prison would be seen as cruel and unusual punishment."

She gave him a wide-eyed, innocent look, but Daniel wasn't buying it for a minute.

"I wouldn't be so sure about that if I were you. And remember, in prison, the inmates can't get their hands on iPads, pizzas, or strawberry milkshakes!"

She immediately grew serious. "Hmm. Good point. I guess I better start behaving around here, and that means kicking my visitors out when visiting hours are over. Goodnight, Daniel."

Daniel scooped up their empty milkshake containers. As he had the previous week, he hid them inside his coat until he could dispose of them where no one would see them. Angel gave him a wink and a little wave.

He smiled, turned, and headed out the door. "Good night, Angel, sleep tight, and don't let the lemon air fresheners bite!" he called out from the hallway.

Daniel walked out, carrying their two empty milkshake containers, his heart full of mixed emotions. His little Angel made him laugh, and she had an uncanny ability for making him forget his troubles for a little while. He'd experienced a real emotional breakthrough tonight, by reliving the accident and unloading his guilt. As weird as it seemed, he was making more progress with a seven-year-old kid than he did with the court-appointed psychiatrist. Angel spoke in simple terms, but her philosophies on love and life touched him at a deeper level. She was right; he could not change the past, and he had to accept that everything happens for a reason, including the tragic accident that had totally changed his life.

Although it might be a challenge for him, in order to heal and move on with his life, he had to forgive himself. And it sure couldn't hurt to try following Angel's advice. Maybe if he repeated the Forgiveness Luvffirmation often enough, the whole process would move a lot faster. Somehow, he needed to see the bigger picture, and he was optimistic that Angel was going to help him open his eyes to the next big chapter in his life. Crazy idea…how could a seven-year-old, sick child have such a huge impact? But for some reason, he felt sure she would.

*****

That following week might have been the easiest Daniel had experienced in at least two years. He made it a point to be friendly and continued to surprise his co-workers by participating in conversations and showing his boss he could be a real "team player." That Tuesday, even his parole officer seemed impressed with Daniel's attitude. Although he still told the man what he thought the officer wanted to hear, Daniel injected his answers with optimism and friendliness. Later that week, he went to his mom's again—this time, she served meatloaf stuffed with Swiss cheese and mushrooms—and they talked more…about his ideas for his future and how he planned to make a better life for himself.

"I want to be in a position to take care of you in your old age," he told her. "You shouldn't have to slave away until you're ninety years old."

His mom had laughed and given him a big hug. "That's really kind of you," she said. "But I've been building a pension for the last twenty years. By the time I retire, I should be okay. You just need to worry about your own self. Get a job that makes you happy…find a good woman…settle down, and maybe give me a few grand-babies to spoil rotten."

"Grand babies!" Daniel forced a laugh, a little uncomfortable with the idea. Not to mention, her statement about finding a good woman made his heart hurt a little and brought back memories of a love he'd lost. "Mom, I'm like, twenty-one years old." As far as he was concerned, he wouldn't be having any children for a long, long time. He had other priorities right now...

She'd agreed with him but told him not to wait too long. She wanted to still be young enough to take them to the playground and enjoy their company.

As he'd bid her good-night, he'd already been looking forward to next week's dinner. Not only was she an amazing cook—at this rate, he'd gain back the weight he'd lost in prison in a hurry—she was also a good friend. And as he compared her mood these last couple weeks with how she'd been since he'd gone to jail, he realized *his* depression had caused *her* to be down in the dumps. When he was hurting, she felt his pain. When he shed tears, she felt his sadness, and the reverse was also true. For her—and for himself—he had to get his act together. And Daniel had a feeling Angel would play a big role in him doing exactly that...

WEEK 5

Daniel took the stairs to the third floor of the hospice two at a time. He smiled with confidence as he passed a couple of nurses standing near the door to another patient's room on his way down the corridor to see Angel. The milkshakes he'd bought were carefully hidden away in a bright red-and-white striped gift bag this time. He'd even added a red bow and ribbon tied to the handles and figured Angel could use the bag to hold some of her special treasures she had sitting around on her table. He paused at her door, took a deep breath, then burst inside the room.

"Happy Friday! Did someone order milkshakes?" he asked cheerfully. He frowned and looked around the room. "Angel?"

The bed was empty, the room completely silent. He took a couple tentative steps toward the bathroom, listening for any signs of his little Angel. Damn, he hoped she wasn't sick again. The door was partially closed.

"Angel?" he repeated. He didn't want to disturb her if she were…busy in there. "Oh, Angel…are you here?"

His questions were met with silence, so he pulled open the door and glanced inside.

Letting out a sigh of relief at finding the bathroom empty, he turned and scowled. Where could she be? As far as he knew, they never did any kinds of tests or treatments on Friday evenings, so she *should* be there in her bed. Had she gotten sick again and maybe needed some kind of special…? He shrugged. Daniel had no idea what they might do for her if she were feeling really ill. Did they have a certain area of the hospice where they took kids who were too sick for visitors?

He made his way back out into the hall and paused, listening. The sound of children's laughter echoed along the corridor. If he recalled correctly from his initial tour, there was a family visiting room down the other end somewhere, and the noise seemed to be coming from there. He headed in that direction. If Angel wasn't there, maybe someone would know where she was. The two nurses he'd seen on his way in had disappeared, and he wasn't about to bother any of the other patients.

He paused at the open door to the visitors' area, cringing as one little boy shrieked with high-pitched laughter.

"Look! Another birthday present for Angel," a bright-eyed little girl squealed. She jumped up and down, pointing at the bag in Daniel's hand.

Oh, shoot. Oh, crap. What had he just walked himself into? And where in the *heck* was Angel? He craned his neck, searching from one side of the room to the other, trying to see over the heads of what seemed to Daniel to be a small army of little kids, all of them crowding around in front of him now.

"Mattie, Sam, Ferdinand, Bobby," a familiar little voice called out. "Will you guys move aside and let my friend Daniel come all the way into the room, please?"

Several of the children in front of Daniel stepped out of the way, and there sat Angel at one of those cafeteria-style tables—the kind with the benches connected to the table at the bottom so you can't move them in and sit closer or rearrange them in any way. A few colorfully wrapped packages and gift bags sat on the table in front of her, and another half dozen children or so were sitting or standing beside and behind her. She had on one of those plastic crowns little girls use to play dress-up, and she looked up at him and grinned.

"Hey, Danny-Boy!" She gave him a little wave. "Come on in, and sit with us, won't you?"

Like a queen holding court, visiting with her royal subjects, Angel appeared perfectly at ease. She definitely didn't look any sicker than she usually did—thank goodness. But what was going on here, exactly? A couple of nurses sat at another table in the far back corner of the room, and so far, they didn't act as if they'd noticed his arrival. At least, neither of them had looked his way. They appeared deep in conversation, their heads together, speaking in hushed tones. As quietly and unobtrusively as possible, Daniel made his way over to Angel.

"Hey, kid," he said, leaning over and speaking so only she and those closest to them could hear. "I didn't know it was your birthday." His cheeks grew warm. Why hadn't she told him about this during his last visit? He could have stopped and gotten her something special.

"But, mister, you brought her a *present*," piped up a brown-haired little boy, his curious gaze zeroing in on the bag in Daniel's hand.

"Oh, yeah…" He lifted the gift bag and glanced at it before turning back to Angel. "Well, actually, this isn't really a birthday present because I didn't know it was her birthday today."

Daniel looked back at the table where the two tired-looking nurses still sat. He assumed they were here to keep an eye on things…maybe help with the party and watch the kids…but where were the parents? Other friends or relatives? Wouldn't Angel have more people at her birthday party than just her fellow patients? He glanced back at her and nervously waited for her cue. He had no idea what he should do with the gift bag that contained what the hospice staff would definitely consider a prohibited substance. Daniel cringed inwardly, feeling like some kind of drug smuggler or something.

Her eyes sparkling mischievously, Angel replied to his request for help. "Ah, Daniel, how *nice* of you to bring me a *present* for my birthday. I guess you must have received my email invitation. Please, bring it here; I can't wait to see what you got me."

Daniel's cheeks grew even hotter. What the heck was she doing? She had to know what was in the bag. And what was that about an email invitation? Angel knew darn well Daniel couldn't access the Internet, so how—? Oh… The solution hit him, and he shook his head at her. Rotten brat. Obviously, she was messing with him, and she was taking delight in making him squirm. But geez, didn't she know what was at stake? If the nurses discovered the milkshakes, they would take them away; he would get into trouble with the hospice staff and perhaps even with his parole officer for violating a hospice rule. This could get serious, and yet, Angel just sat there with a smirk on her little face. *Okay*, he thought; *let the games begin*. He stepped closer to his opponent and handed her the gift bag.

"Here you go, Angel, happy birthday. I think you're going to love your gift…berry, berry much."

A couple of the kids who'd stood close enough to hear his comment looked at him oddly, but most of the children cheered with joy. No doubt, they were excited to see what was in the bag. All the noise must have caught the nurses' attention, finally, because they stopped chatting and turned his way. They both leaned closer, looking back and forth between Daniel and the gift bag. As for Angel, her expression shifted from smugness to concern, and she glared at Daniel. He smirked, wondering what she'd do next. She'd started this little contest of wills, but Daniel intended to finish it.

He watched her closely and could practically see her mind working. Would she realize the consequences if the kids—and more importantly, the nurses—discovered the two strawberry milkshakes hidden in the gift bag? Of course, the nurses would confiscate them, and heaven forbid, they might even drink them! Daniel would most likely get into trouble for violating the hospice rules regarding no outside food for the sick kids. Since he was on probation and doing community service work, he might even get banned from the hospice. Would the thought of losing a good friend and cutting off her supply of milkshakes make her concede this time and give up their little game of bluff and dare?

"Hey, guys," Angel said suddenly, "I'm not feeling too well. I think I better head back to my room."

Daniel grinned. Smart girl! He coughed to cover his laughter at her skillful ploy. "That's a good idea," he told her, feigning concern. "I can help you if you like."

The other kids sounded their displeasure, and they begged Angel to open her last birthday gift. The nurses had gotten up from their table and tried to quiet the excited kids.

"That's enough, now," one nurse said, holding out her arms as if to round up all the children. "You've had your fun for the day. Angel's not feeling well. You can find out what her friend brought for her some other time…"

"Angel, please make certain you take everything with you," the other nurse said wearily. "The hospice can't be responsible if you leave something here and it goes missing."

Daniel had to hide his smug smile behind a mask of concern, taking great pleasure in knowing he had just schooled his teacher and beat her at her own game. In a show of good sportsmanship, he helped her gather up her things, and he offered to escort her back to her room. He knew she was looking forward to opening and drinking her present in private. He wouldn't mind a strawberry milkshake right about then, either, and if they didn't get moving, the darn things would be melted and not nearly as good. Just as they were getting ready to go, Angel paused.

"Thank you, Daniel," she said, speaking loudly and clearly enough for all the children and the nurses to hear her, "for the thoughtful present. I'll be sure to show the kids and the nurses my beautiful gift tomorrow morning."

And with those words, Angel won their little game. She looked up at Daniel with her victory smile plastered on her face. Now he would be expected to bring her a real present so she could show off his generosity to the curious kids and the monitoring nurses. At least, she had given him about twelve hours to shop, wrap, and deliver her present by morning. Daniel followed her in silence and in awe to her room. This kid was not only wise; she knew how to play to win. Once they were seated together on the bed, they slurped their milkshakes and giggled about the game they'd just played.

"I totally underestimated you," he admitted. "You're a mischievous devil trapped in an Angel's body. I hope the other kids aren't too disappointed they had to miss the opening of your gift bag."

"They'll be fine…" Angel took another long sip of her shake and sighed a happy-sounding sigh. "Besides"—she flashed him a grin—"they'll get to see the beautiful present you're going to deliver tomorrow."

Daniel shook his head. "You're a bad little angel sometimes, you know that, right?" He laughed. "I'll do my best to surprise you and your friends tomorrow. You're lucky it's Friday, and I don't have to work."

"Speaking of which," she said, "how was your week?"

He set his now-empty shake container on the floor beside the chair and leaned forward. "I think you'll be proud of me, Angel. I wore my red love wristband all week long, I repeated the Forgiveness Luvffirmation as often as I could, I had a *great* dinner date with my mom—that woman is going to make me *fat* by the way—*and* I was aware of my so-called *love switch*." Daniel grinned self-consciously. "It wasn't on all the time, but I knew when it switched off, and I made an effort to turn it back on."

A month ago, if anyone had told him he'd be doing any of those things, he'd have said they were crazy. *Forgiveness Luvffirmations? Love switches?* He would have laughed his head off. Even when he'd first done as Angel had suggested, that first week with the Luvffirmation, he'd mostly only listened to her to humor a sick, little kid. But once he'd tried, and once he'd noticed a difference, he'd stuck with it because he wanted to keep feeling better.

"Wow, Grasshopper, you are mastering the lessons."

"Ha! Grasshopper, is it? What are you, my sensei now? I didn't know you were teaching me martial arts or that I was supposed to be your grasshopper."

"Sorry…" She sighed and lay back against the stack of pillows. "I get super bored sometimes, and the other day, I was streaming old, martial arts movies. I thought it was funny that the student was referred to as 'Grasshopper'. In a way, I guess we are all transforming in our lives—maybe less like grasshoppers, since they don't complete their metamorphosis, and more like…butterflies." She paused and grinned. "You're transforming, too, from someone who repelled love to someone who gives off loving vibes. Did you know grasshoppers only live from three to five months? And some butterflies live only a week! The monarch lives about nine months, but that's 'cause it's bigger. They naturally know that life is too short *not* to transform. Imagine if the caterpillar didn't emerge into a beautiful butterfly. The natural cycle in the world would be upset, and nature would be out of balance." She paused, cocked her head, and gave him a look. "Which brings me to a question I have for you… Do you think our world is out of balance, Danny-Boy?"

Daniel blinked. He'd been listening closely to her soft, serious voice, absorbing her words, and, as usual, she shocked him with her mature, philosophical vision. He had to keep reminding himself he was listening to a seven-year-old child. Still…butterflies and grasshoppers?

He shrugged. "I guess so, Angel, but I find the comparison to grasshoppers and butterflies a bit far-fetched. We're not insects, and we don't just buzz around all day. We're way more advanced, don't you think?"

Angel laughed and slapped her thigh. "Obviously, you've never seen New York City during rush hour from a bird's-eye point of view!"

"And you have?" He interrupted her. "Well-travelled, are you?"

"Well, I've only been there once. When I was first diagnosed, Mom and I flew to Sloan-Kettering for a second opinion."

Ugh! Daniel had to learn to keep his big mouth shut. He hated reminding Angel of her illness, even if he'd done so unintentionally. "Sorry…"

"For what? You had no way of knowing." She gave him a soft smile. "Anyway, if you look from a high-soaring eagle's perspective—or like I did, from the window of a jet airplane—humans look like a bunch of insects buzzing here, there, and everywhere. You would notice some faster-moving yellow ones and some slower-moving, two-legged ones. Now, imagine if all of those city insects transformed into loving beings. With such an emergence of their natural love state, they would help restore the natural balance in the world."

"Okay… I have to ask; what kind of medication are you on tonight?"

"Oh, don't you worry, Daniel." She shook her head and frowned. "I'm only taking the doctor-prescribed pharmaceuticals with all of those lovely side effects. You know the ones—might cause severe nausea, weight-loss, and baldness." She brightened and sat forward, touching her blonde wig. "By the way, did you notice the new green streak I added to my hair? Maybe I'm transforming into a green bug, Danny-Boy." She giggled, sounding her age for a change. "But to answer your question, I *am* flying a bit high today because of my birthday celebration."

He nodded. "Totally understandable, but I'll be honest with you, kid, I'm having a hard time relating to your bug analogies."

She sighed and shook her head. "Let me see if I can explain better. Have you ever seen a firefly, Danny-Boy? They're one of my favorite bugs and one of my best memories of playing outside at our family's cabin. They lit up the forest at night. My brother and I had a blast, catching them and putting them in a glass container. They would light up the jar like a flashlight, and then we would release them back into the darkness. Fireflies could probably light up the whole forest if they all turned their lights on at the same time. Do you see where I am going with this, Daniel?"

"Yeah, I suppose. I can imagine the bugs lighting up the night. I'm just not sure where this lesson is going, but please continue, my sensei."

Angel put her hands together in front of her, palms facing, and gave him a little bow. "Very good, Grasshopper, you are an honorable student," she said in a very bad imitation of an Asian accent. "Now, please bring your attention back to New York City, and imagine if all of those insects were fireflies. Visualize that it is night time, and the city officials have ordered all of the lights to be turned off. Picture the perfect blackout scenario, where there is no visible light. Now, cast your attention like a fly fisherman, focusing on the insects. What would NYC look like if ten percent of the fireflies lit up at the same time, or twenty-five percent, or fifty percent, or maybe even one hundred percent? The city would light up as more and more fireflies turned their lights on together. I hope you're still with me, Danny-Boy, because this bug analogy is about to get a little creepy."

Daniel laughed. "Sweetie, you couldn't possible creep me out any more than some of the things I've seen and heard over the last couple of years. Nothing *but nothing* is creepier than hearing the cockroaches in prison. They only came out at night, and they would scurry under our beds, and sometimes, we would find them under our sheets."

"Eew, oh my gosh, that's gross! Okay, you definitely creeped me out with that one! I can't *stand* cockroaches." She sighed and shook her head. "It's too bad there weren't any fireflies to enlighten you in prison."

"Punny, very punny, Angel."

"Yeah, I guess that was pretty good." She grinned. "But I'm trying to be serious here, Daniel. Imagine if we gave off light when our love switch was turned on, like fireflies do when they're lighting up the night. We would have the potential to light up ourselves, our homes, the city we live in, our country, and ultimately, the entire planet. Have you seen the satellite images of the Earth at night? They show small clusters of lights in the countryside and bright concentrations of lights in the major cities. These artificial light sources are bright, but they are not as powerful as the natural illumination of love." She gave him another one of those calm, steady, penetrating looks. "So, here's one more question for you; are you ready to help light up the world with love?"

Daniel sat quietly for a moment, thinking over his answer. As much as he wanted to tell her what she wanted to hear—that yes, he was ready to do whatever she needed him to do—he couldn't. He just couldn't. At least, not yet. "To be honest, Angel, I'm not sure if I'm ready to light up myself, never mind help light up the entire world."

She leaned forward again and patted his knee. "That's okay because I'm going to show you how to turn on your love switch, and keep it on. Once your love switch is turned on, you'll give off light naturally…just like a great, big firefly on a beautiful, starry night. Do you know how fireflies light up or why they light up, Danny-Boy?"

Geez. Was there any subject this kid didn't know something about? He shook his head. "No, I don't, but I have a feeling you and Pinky are about to educate me on the subject of entomology."

"Yep. We sure are." She grinned. "I have been bugging my friends with my insect wisdom, and I'll be happy to pester—I mean *educate* you, too. Fireflies never need to worry about replacing a light bulb or paying the electric bill. They are powered by something called bioluminescence—

"Another big word for a little girl," he said. One she hadn't even struggled to pronounce. Daniel frowned. Her intelligence seemed to know no bounds and was a little…disconcerting. "You can't tell me you learned all this from a simple Google search."

Angel smiled a mysterious smile. "A firefly's light source is totally internal. Every blink of light is created by a chemical reaction between three things—luciferase, which is a kind of protein, luciferin, which is a pigment, and oxygen. When combined, the result is a bright, little light. Most bioluminescent critters always glow, kind of like a light bulb that never goes off. But fireflies are special—they can turn their lights on and off. What do you think about that, Danny-Boy? Maybe the light switch is actually their love switch?"

"I'm not sure if you're my teacher or my sensei or Siri or perhaps a blend of all three." He shook his head. She sure sounded like she had the mind of a computer. Maybe she had a photographic memory or was some kind of child prodigy or something? "Okay, Siri, if fireflies have a light or a love switch, why do they turn it on and off?"

"Well, I'm glad you asked, Mr. Daniel," she said brightly. "In adult fireflies, most researchers think bioluminescence has a couple different purposes—to attract a mate and to attract prey. Firefly flashes happen super fast…in the blink of an eye…and we might not be able to see the difference, but lady fireflies know exactly what to look for. Apparently, some lady fireflies want a male that has the longest flash, while others prefer males that flash the fastest."

"Thank you, Siri, but didn't your mom warn you that you can't always believe what you read online?" Daniel had to wonder about the amount of time she spent online and what else she might be learning from the often-ugly world in cyberspace.

"Of course. But I'm telling you, this stuff is true. Recent research has proven two things. One…fireflies turn their light switch on when they are feeling the love, and two, girl fireflies are a lot like human girls—we *loves* us some flashy males!"

"Hey, you're only seven years old," he reminded her with a scowl. "You're not supposed to be interested in flashy males. Flashy insects, yes, but not flashy boys!"

"Yeah, well, if you only had a few months to live, wouldn't you be interested in searching for love?" she asked and then went on before he had a chance to respond. "Besides, during my online research on flashy male fireflies, I found some pretty cool stuff related to cancer research. Some of the scientists who researched the fireflies found the thing in the firefly's DNA that's responsible for producing luciferase. The put this light-producing gene into the cells of other animals and found out they can see those particular cells. The medical community thought this was a very amazing and exciting discovery. Think about it; maybe one day, they'll be able to make cancer cells glow, which would make it a lot easier to find out how different cancer treatments work. Imagine if they implanted the light-producing gene in my cancer-ridden body? I would light up like a firefly, and do you know why my light would stay on, Daniel?"

He spoke without thinking. "Because life is too short not to love?"

"Exactly! Wow. You're learning fast. And now, Danny-Boy, it's time for you to light up, too!"

Daniel yawned, stretching his arms up in the air and moving his head back and forth to work out the kink in his neck that had developed from sitting there in one spot for so long. "You're right; it is time for me to light up and fly away like a firefly. It's getting late, and I have to get up early to go shopping for someone special."

Angel gave him what he'd come to recognize as her fake pouty face. "Oh, Daniel, I'm sorry you have to go. But I agree—you do have an important mission tomorrow morning, and I hope it's a surprising success!" She grabbed his hand and held tight. "But before you go, please—just give me two more minutes. I want to help you light up with love this week. Earlier, you mentioned that you were aware when your love switch was off, and that's great—it's the first step in the process, and too many people walk around in a state of unhappy unawareness. Most people don't have a clue why they feel sad, lonely, moody, angry, fearful, and all of those other dark feelings. If only they knew how to switch on the power of love in their lives. The light of love would brighten their dark feelings, and like a firefly, they would give off some much-needed love and light in the world." She gave his hand a quick squeeze. "Daniel, if I teach you, you could teach others. We could work together to help light up the world with love."

Instead of becoming inspired by Angel's questions and comments tonight, Daniel felt oddly depressed. If he were totally honest with himself and with her, he didn't think he could live up to her expectations. "Angel, you have lofty goals for a young girl. I don't think I've ever met anyone as positive or inspiring as you are, but I'm not you… I don't think I'm the kind of guy who could inspire others. My dark past will always be in my shadow, no matter how much love and light I produce. I don't mean to disappoint you, but I hope you can understand what I'm telling you. I just don't think I can be who you want me to be."

He started to pull away, but she held firm. Apparently, she wasn't willing to give up on him quite yet.

"Do you believe in love, Daniel? Are you aware of the power of love, of the unlimited power of unconditional love? Have you ever loved someone unconditionally or felt the unconditional love of a pet or maybe from Sox? How about your girlfriend? You loved her, didn't you?"

Daniel closed his eyes briefly and sucked in a deep breath as pain constricted his chest. He couldn't go there. Not tonight. As gently as he could, he removed his hand from hers and took a step back. "You ask a lot of questions for a tired kid." He quickly changed the subject. "By the way, why didn't you tell me it was your birthday?"

"Oh, I see; this is your way of avoiding answering the love questions. Well, Daniel, if you *must* know, it wasn't my birthday today. The nurses like to host monthly birthday celebrations for the kids who are terminally ill." She shrugged then looked down. "I guess it's their way of making us feel special." She glanced back up at him and grinned. "And thanks to you, Danny-Boy, I feel very special because I get birthday presents two days in a row!"

Wow. The idea of throwing a birthday party "just for the fun of it" for a kid who was going to die soon brought a lump to Daniel's throat.

"Yes," he said, "you're very special, and that's why I have to go—so I can shop for a special gift for a special kid." He turned, intending to leave.

"Oh, no you don't. You're not getting off that easy, Daniel."

He spun around. What now?

"Unless you want me to push the nurses' call button?" she asked him. "I'm sure they'd love to know what was in the gift bag tonight."

Blackmail? She wouldn't dare. He gave her a fierce scowl. "Well, it's a good thing we sucked down all the evidence then, isn't it?"

"Unfortunately for you, Danny-Boy, our nurses have a great sense of smell, and they could sniff out the evidence in our empty cups from two rooms away! So, why don't we visit for just a little while longer, and then you can take the evidence home with you? I don't mean to pry, but I'm curious about your experiences with love. What happened to your girlfriend, Daniel?" She sat forward, elbows on her knees, chin in her palms, obviously preparing to listen.

Daniel thought a minute. Why not tell her? He'd shared just about everything else. He cleared his mind and focused on the facts, but his voice still quivered with emotion. "I lost all contact with her after the accident. Her parents made sure our relationship was over, and they her sent her away to college and far away from me. We were high school sweethearts, and when she left, she took a piece of my heart with her. To be honest, it was probably the best thing for both of us. We were too young to understand love, and after the accident, I was not capable of loving anyone. So, long story short, to answer your question, she is gone, and I am not expecting her to come back."

Angel sighed. "That's sad," she said, "but it's also an important lesson for you. Did you notice how you felt just now, when you shared the story about losing your girlfriend? You turned your love switch off just by thinking about your long-lost love. Can you see how easy it is for people to switch their love on and off based on their personal experiences? Our challenge is to keep our love on, regardless of the conditions in our lives."

"Yes, Dr. Angel," he teased her. "But that's a big challenge for me, and I'm sure it's a challenge for others who have experienced bad things in their lives, too. How am I supposed to keep my *love switch* on when I feel stuck in a reoccurring *nightmare* filled with guilt, fear, and shame?" The more he spoke, the less light-hearted he felt, and even he heard the melancholy in his voice.

"Oh, Daniel…" Angel climbed down off the bed, came to stand before him, and took his hand. "You're not alone, you know? Our world is trapped in a dark nightmare. Fortunately, the alarm bells are ringing and signaling us to wake up and usher in the light. It's time for us fireflies to band together with our love lights turned on. Are you ready to take flight?"

He glanced up and away from her penetrating, blue-eyed gaze. "I don't know. You keep asking me if I am ready to turn my love on, or if I can help light up the world with love, or if I can fly around like a firefly." He looked back down at her. "But sometimes, I feel more like a creepy cockroach than a flashy firefly."

Angel cocked her head and grinned. "Am I *bugging* you, Daniel?"

He didn't laugh at her attempt at a joke. "Oh, you are just *so punny* tonight, aren't you? These are pretty serious, stressful topics you're bringing up, and, yeah, to be honest with you, your analogy to insects is bugging me. Maybe we're more like a swarm of bees, buzzing around and stinging those who get in our way. What do you think about that, *honey*?"

Angel nodded. "Good one, Daniel. That was a real stinger. I might be too young and innocent to talk about the birds and the bees, but we can still chat about your lack of a love life. You mentioned that your girlfriend will probably never come back. During my online love research, I discovered an interesting quote that went something like this: 'if you love someone, set them free, and if they return, then it was meant to be'. If she ever does return, would you be able to love her unconditionally?"

Daniel started to tell her it didn't matter; his ex-girlfriend wasn't ever coming back, but Angel held up a hand and cut him off.

"You don't need to answer *that* question right now, but I would love to hear you complete this sentence: 'I have to learn to love myself unconditionally first before I can…?'"

Thankful to be back on firmer ground, at least so far as the topic of conversation was concerned, Daniel nodded. "All right, all right, I guess this is a test to see if I have been paying attention in class?"

She smiled that big, beaming smile of hers. "Yep!"

"Okay, Miss Angel, here you go... I have to learn to love myself unconditionally before I can love others unconditionally."

Angel jumped up and down a little and clapped excitedly. "Yay, I'm so proud of you, Danny-Boy! You've passed your first test in the game of love. Sox would be proud of you, too, especially if you still love her unconditionally like you did when you were a kid."

"I love Sox just like you love Red—unconditionally—but of course, it's a heck of a lot easier to love our stuffed animals. There's no risk involved. They can't hurt us, and we can't hurt them or disappoint them, either."

Angel glanced at the clock above the door. "You still have plenty of time before the bus comes. Will you *please* come sit down for just another few minutes?" She swayed on her feet. "I'm getting a little dizzy."

Daniel took her arm to steady her. Knowing Angel, she wouldn't let him leave until she'd had her say, and Daniel didn't want to make her stand there talking to him any longer than necessary. "Sure. Let's get you back to bed."

He escorted her and helped her climb back up into the bed, then he slumped down in the blue vinyl chair again.

Once Angel had gotten comfortable, pillows propped against the wood and metal headboard, she sighed. "That's better. Now...where were we?" She smiled. "Oh, yeah, you're right about our stuffed animals. We can't hurt them emotionally. But they can awaken our capacity to love. We can practice with them...learn how to play the game of love."

"If love is a game, then it sure is challenging to play."

"Life is a game of love, and when we play nicely together, everyone wins. Unfortunately, too many people think life is a competitive game. How do you play the game of life, Daniel? Do you play to win, or do you play to love?"

Daniel wasn't sure how to answer Angel's questions. He had to keep reminding himself he was having these mature conversations with a kid. While he didn't want to disappoint her, he also didn't want to divulge too much about his personal relationships. He knew he was failing in the game of love. His heart had hardened as a result of the sad and tragic things he'd gone through.

"If you and your girlfriend get back together again, maybe you could play a love game, like Syncrohearts."

"Sychro-what? Angel, where do you *find* these things?"

"Don't worry." She shook her head and laughed. "It's not one of *those* kind of relationship games. It's called the Syncrohearts Love Game, and I found it in the App Store. Supposedly, it helps couples understand each other's hearts, and it looks like a fun game…for adults, I mean. Don't worry; I didn't download it onto Pinky. I just read the description. I wish I could tell Mom about it… I think my parents deserve some fun playtime together." Her smile disappeared. "Especially with all the sadness they've had lately."

"I think your dad was right. Kids your age should spend more time playing outside and less time playing online. A seven year old shouldn't have to worry so much about her parents, and she definitely shouldn't have to think about something so huge as bringing about world peace."

"Well, since I'm stuck in this hospice, I don't have many choices. I'll have to entertain myself with Pinky and my other, loftier goals. Besides, doing online searches for love doesn't take me to too many not-suitable-for-minors websites, and I'm getting a lot better at figuring out which ones are which just by reading the Google descriptions."

"Something tells me you broke another one of your mother's rules for using your iPad." Daniel shook his head, cringing as he thought about what some of those website descriptions probably said.

"Oh, I don't think my mom needs to know anything about my online love searches. Although, when she used my iPad, she asked why there were no links in my browser history."

Angel had the good grace to look a bit ashamed. He could tell she didn't exactly like going against her mother's rules.

"And how did you explain that one, Miss Angel?" he asked her.

"I just told her I loved playing the games that were preloaded on my iPad, and I didn't need to search for online games." Again, Angel dipped her head and avoided his gaze.

"You're one crafty kid, but I don't think your mom would approve of your online searches for love games." If her mom and dad didn't know what she was up to, Daniel felt obligated to warn her she was treading on dangerous ground.

Angel sighed. "You're right; I don't need a relationship love game yet, and that wasn't the point of my searches anyway." She made a sound that indicated her frustration. "I've already explained what I think I need—what we all need. Everyone on Earth should be playing a game of love, where our collective goal is to light up the world with love. What do you think, Danny-Boy, do you think the world's population is ready to participate in a global game of love?"

Daniel shrugged. She'd already asked him something similar earlier. "We definitely need to do something to improve the world, but I'm not sure if the general population is ready for a global love game. First of all, how would you get everyone to play? Seems like that would take a heck of a lot of organization."

"When I surf the latest news topics, I get flooded with wave after wave of violence, crime, corruption, terrorism, poverty, tragic accidents, and natural disasters. Sometimes, I feel like unplugging my iPad, pulling up the covers, and hiding away in my bed. Then I wake up and remember that life is too short not to love. We owe it to future generations to counteract all of the depressing, bad news with more inspiring, good news. Besides, a world full of enlightening fireflies would be a lot nicer than a world full of scary cockroaches!" Angel smiled a little, Mona-Lisa smile. "As for how… well, we haven't quite gotten to that point yet, but when we do, you'll be the first to know. I promise!"

"Angel, your philosophies on life are infectious. Have you ever thought about running for political office?" The moment he asked the question, he wanted to bite his tongue off. Although he could see her growing up and holding an important political office, she'd never have that chance. She'd never even have the chance to grow up…

But Angel either didn't mind his faux pas, or she hadn't even considered the implications of his statement because she didn't miss a beat.

"Does that mean I have your vote, or would you prefer to be my campaign manager?" She grinned.

"President Angel has a nice ring to it." He played along with her game.

"Do you believe in God, Daniel?" she suddenly asked.

Daniel had to laugh. "Kid, didn't your parents teach you that politics and religion should not be discussed in social settings?"

"Well, since this is more of a classroom, I think these topics are fair game. Besides, we're talking about love. I believe in God, and I also believe in the power of unconditional love."

Daniel wasn't certain what he believed. He had taken a class on religion in college, and he'd done his own research. "Do you know how many people have died or been persecuted in the name of religion?" he asked her.

"Yes, and that's very sad, but it just proves we need to adopt the basic values of love, respect, tolerance, and compassion. What would our world be like if we loved ourselves and each other unconditionally? I respect all religions, spiritual beliefs, and even atheists. It doesn't mean I agree with other beliefs or opinions, especially those that promote hatred, violence, and fear. Even a seven-year-old kid can figure out we spend too much time comparing, debating, and defending our different beliefs and opinions. I think diversity is good for our world, and I also think we should focus our energies on the one common thing we can all believe in—love! Don't you think that makes more sense?"

"President or preacher, I am not sure which hat you should wear, Angel."

Angel laughed. "I prefer colorful wigs over powerful hats. Although, my grandmother said I was born with angelic powers. Of course, she also said too much candy brought out the devil in me. When I told her, I needed candy to power my angel wings, she reminded me, 'Dear child, love is all the power you'll need'. You would have loved my grandma Daniel. She had a big heart, a beautiful smile, and she gave the best hugs. Sadly, she passed away about a month before I got sick, but I know she would have supported our love mission."

"Unfortunately, I think our world has become too divisive." He really didn't think her idea of world love stood a chance. There were too many people out there who craved money and power above all else—even love…

"Do you love Donald?" she asked.

Daniel shook his head. Donald? "I told you; it's not polite to talk about politics and religion."

"Whoa, wait a minute, who's talking about politics? I thought everyone loved Donald Duck. You know…the popular, Disney cartoon character that has brought lots of love and laughter to millions of people around the world? Did you know Donald Duck was created back in 1934, and he has appeared in more films than any other Disney character?" She went on, sounding more and more like *Encyclopedia Britannica* with every word. "Danny-Boy, if one fun-loving cartoon character can help spread love around the world, think about what we could do collectively."

"Well, love on Donald Duck. Seriously, Angel, what you are talking about can only happen in cartoons."

"And that's exactly why we have to demonstrate the power of unconditional love. Once we start to light up the world with love, love will become contagious." She nodded. "I promise you, I've got this all figured out."

Daniel glanced up at the clock above the door. "Oh, my, look at the time. I guess I better scurry out of here before the nurses sniff out our strawberry milkshake containers and place me in quarantine. We wouldn't want that now, would we?" He leaped to his feet. He'd had more than his fill of philosophical conversation for one night, and she'd given him a lot to think about…plus, he really did need to make that last bus.

"No, I don't want to lose my supplier or my good friend, either. Since I cherish our friendship, I want to send you home with a parting gift that will keep on giving all week long and, hopefully, for the rest of your life! I'm pleased to share a prescription for turning your love on and keeping it on. You will be happy to know this prescription is easy to administer, and it has no side-effects, only positive results!"

Daniel stuffed his hands into his coat pockets and stared down at her. "Why do I get the impression you're trying to nurse me back to love, regardless of my capacity to love?"

"Trust me, Daniel, your capacity to love is going to grow with this prescription. The daily use of the Luvffirmations will help ignite the healing power of love from within. The essential ingredient of love was added to an affirmation format to create the Luvffirmations. They are simple, easy to use, and they are very powerful, like the one I shared with you a few weeks ago for forgiving and loving yourself: *I am love, and I forgive and love myself.* They work miracles, and I know this from personal experience. As I told you earlier, I had to learn to forgive before I could learn to love."

He nodded. "The forgiveness Luvffirmation seems to be working for me, too, but I am a bit skeptical of things like this."

"I know that. But if you can keep an open mind and an open heart, the Luvffirmations will help open you up to unconditional love. Here is your parting gift: *I am love, and I value and love myself unconditionally, and I value and love others unconditionally, too.* I encourage you to repeat this Luvffirmation as often as you can, especially if your thoughts start to drift to the darker, cockroach-infested corners of your mind."

"Thank you for sharing your love insights, and I promise I will do the best I can." He couldn't really give her more than that, although he sensed she knew he had a long way to go and was willing to be patient.

"By the way, why did you get disconnected from technology, Danny-Boy? Was that part of your punishment, too?" she asked, her voice soft and gentle.

He sighed. "Yes. I'm afraid so, and I guess it makes sense, considering the circumstances surrounding my accident." He nodded toward her head. "Now, you owe me an explanation on your rainbow-colored hair, but I'm tired, so we can save that conversation for next time."

She looked thoughtful for a moment then nodded. "Okay, Daniel, I guess our next visit will be in techno color!"

He turned and headed out the door, calling over his shoulder as he left. "Good night, Angel, sleep tight, and don't let the colorful cockroaches bite!"

"Eeeew!"

Daniel laughed all the way down the back staircase.

*****

Daniel awoke Saturday morning with the birthday-gift mission playing out in his head. He knew exactly what his little Angel deserved, and he was excited about his next move in their little game. He happily delivered the large package to the nurses' station, and he slipped away before his opponent could engage him.

Angel was taking her morning stroll down the hospice corridor—a daily ritual she'd developed just to get her out of the bed every morning—when she spotted the package perched on the nurses' desk. The "happy birthday" tag confirmed that Daniel had followed through with his game-losing commitment. She happily lugged the big present to her room and then proceeded to rip apart the wrapping. She smiled with pride when she uncovered a second professionally wrapped box within the first box. Daniel's growing sense of humor was a positive sign of his healing. She carefully opened the second box and soon discovered a third box awaiting her patience. She shook her head, wondering how much satisfaction Daniel was getting out of playing this silly game. She took her time opening the third wrapped box, and she was relieved to finally uncover a cylindrical-shaped gift covered in tissue paper. To her surprise, she revealed the game-winning birthday gift—a can of strawberry-scented air freshener. Angel hoped Daniel was giggling as much as she was.

Daniel didn't care if the other passengers thought he was nuts. As the bus pulled away from the curb, he couldn't control the fit of laughter that bubbled up inside him. One thing about Angel…she had an amazing sense of humor—sometimes silly, like that of a kid, and sometimes more sophisticated, like that of an adult. The thought of her smile as she finally uncovered her strawberry-scented gift had him giggling like a crazy person. The people sitting near him glanced his way, no doubt thinking he'd lost his mind, but Daniel just laughed harder. He couldn't recall the last time he'd allowed himself to let loose like that in public, but he felt good. Maybe he was really coming out of the darkness that had dogged him these past years.

Usually, Angel amazed him with her wisdom, and most of the time, she seemed much more thoughtful and even smarter than him. He hated to admit it—even to himself—but he felt kind of proud of himself for defeating her in this little game of hers. Then again, she had all week to plot and plan how she might get back at him. He slumped down in the bus seat, wondering how she might make him pay for his little joke. But instead of worrying, he found Angel's words of advice flowing through his mind.

I am love, and I value and love myself unconditionally, and I value and love others unconditionally, too.

The Luvffirmation echoed in his head throughout the remainder of his bus ride home. As he stepped down onto the sidewalk, Daniel was grinning again. Whatever Angel came up with couldn't be too bad, and the good she brought to his life far outweighed any retribution she might dish out later.

His relationship with her was becoming stronger—and a little weirder—each week. If he closed his eyes, he would see her as some sort of an adult mentor, but then her childish, teasing behavior would suddenly appear. She stirred his emotions, she uncovered his fears, she opened his heart, she inspired his mind, and above all, she'd brought laughter back into his life again. She was becoming his best friend and his best form of therapy. His mundane existence was being recharged with a sense of purpose. He was learning to forgive, he was learning to love, and he was learning about fireflies and rare types of kids' cancer. Angel was a unique child with special gifts that transcended her age and her terminal illness.

Maybe she's my very own, little, guardian angel? He thought, as he let himself into his tiny apartment.

His smile slipped. Before very long, Angel would be gone. Unless a miracle happened, the cancer would claim her, just as it did hundreds or maybe thousands of other little kids each year. His Angel would become a real angel in heaven, and he'd never see her again.

Daniel went from living room to kitchen to bedroom to bathroom, turning on all the lights, hoping to drive away the dark thoughts playing in his mind. He couldn't think about what life might be like without his Friday-evening visits with his new friend. As he sank down on the lumpy, second-hand couch he'd gotten at the local Goodwill store, he wished Angel had given him some kind of Luvffirmation to help ward off the sadness weighing on his heart at that moment.

"Maybe she won't die," he told himself. But he knew better. "Maybe she'll live longer than the doctors say she will." But considering how she looked—a little paler, a little skinnier—that was probably a pretty big "maybe."

What would Angel tell him to do about this horrible, sinking feeling in his heart and the pain in his stomach and chest? Her sweet voice filled his mind.

Make the best of things. Take advantage of every moment. Love life. Focus on the good times, on the things you can control, and let go of the rest…

Daniel nodded. Yeah, that sounded exactly like something Angel would say. She'd definitely kick him in the butt for sitting around moping like this. After all, what good could come from him dwelling on gloomy thoughts? Wasn't the whole point of life to work to make things better? If Angel only had a few weeks or months to live, then Daniel owed it to her to be the best person he could be and to make her final hours on Earth special, in whatever way he could. Yes, she loved the strawberry milkshakes he brought her, but surely, he could come up with some other ways to show her how amazing and important she was and add some sunshine to her life.

*****

The following days flew by, as time tends to do when people are participating in activities they enjoy with people they really like and appreciate. Looking forward to his and Angel's Friday-night visits kept Daniel in a good mood and motivated him throughout the week. At times, his determination to follow her advice and maintain a happy, positive attitude was tested—especially when memories of the accident assaulted him, the horror of that event flashing through his mind in living color. However, he kept his promise, and he repeated the Luvffirmations as Angel had encouraged him to do. He trusted her, and deep down inside, he was learning to trust himself. If his intuition was correct, then he was on the right path to help heal his emotional wounds. Self-healing was an important first step in his recovery, but he sensed Angel had higher expectations for him. If he was going to help "light up the world with love," then he needed to light up like a firefly and quit crawling around in life like a cockroach.

And despite his earlier complaints to Angel, Daniel had to admit, the "bug analogy" seemed to fit. He *was* going through a metamorphosis of sorts, shedding his hard-cased shell and emerging as a more caring person. His heart seemed lighter, his body and mind healthier, and he was seeing the world through a magnified lens of compassion.

Daniel's attitude toward his community service had changed completely. He never saw the visits to the hospice as a duty or obligation or something he *had* to do. In fact, he wished he had more time to spend there, not less. His relationship with Angel had begun to give new meaning to his life.

WEEK 6

"Angel?" Daniel whispered from just inside the door to her room. "Hey, kid...are you asleep? Can I turn the lights on?"

When he didn't get a response, he crept over to the bed. Angel had the covers pulled all the way up over her head, and she didn't appear to be moving. In the shadowy darkness, Daniel's heart started to race as he squinted at the lump on the bed, looking for the telltale rise and fall of the blanket that would indicate she was breathing. She never went to sleep this early. In fact, she always begged him to stay on past visiting hours, even when she looked as if she were ready to pass out sitting up. Maybe she'd had a really busy day and had decided to take a nap before he got there... Or maybe she wasn't feeling well? He'd brought their favorite drinks, safely hidden away in a gym bag that was slung over his shoulder. He'd also stopped at a little store that sold art supplies and had picked up a few other gifts for her, and he couldn't wait to see her face when he gave them to her.

Stacked in the corner on the other side of the bed were three unwrapped gift boxes—the ones he'd put together when he'd given her the air freshener—and he grinned. His gift was nowhere in sight, but he figured she'd put it in her bathroom.

"Angel?"

He moved a couple steps closer. Still no response. His concern increased. The room was eerily quiet, and he wished she'd wake up or at least shift in her sleep a little so he'd know she was okay.

Panicking thoughts swirled in his mind as he reached out to touch her. What if...what if she still didn't move? He paused with his fingertips mere inches from what he assumed was her shoulder. Should he press the emergency call button now? His throat grew tight, and his eyes began to sting. He blinked rapidly to clear them. Hand shaking, he gave her the lightest of nudges.

"Surprise!" Angel flipped back the covers and bolted upright.

Daniel leaped back, crashing into the little nightstand beside the bed. His gym bag flew off his shoulder and landed several feet away on the floor. Angel's mouth fell open, and her eyes went wide.

With one hand pressed to his chest as if he could still his racing heart, Daniel scowled. "Angel, you little bitch! What were you thinking? I thought you were...were *gone*!"

"Tsk-tsk." Angel shook her head. "Such language. Is that any way to speak to a seven-year-old, little kid?" She glanced over at his book bag. "Uh-oh. Look what you did! Quick—you better clean it up before one of the nurses comes in here and discovers that mess."

Daniel stared down in disbelief. The gym bag was on the floor. One container was still intact, but the other one was leaking pink, strawberry milkshake on the clean tile floor. He wanted to ask Angel what would make her pull such a cruel and scary prank on him, but that conversation would have to wait. He didn't want the nurses discovering the evidence of his contraband, so he jumped into action, racing into the bathroom for a handful of paper towels. Angel directed the cleanup efforts from the comfort of her bed, as Daniel dashed back and forth from the bathroom to the bedroom with handfuls of soggy napkins.

"The floor's as clean as it was, but you'll have to spray the room with my new air freshener." Angel nodded toward the bathroom. "It's in there on the counter."

"Why do I have to spray the air freshener?"

"Because if anyone comes in here—or even passes by in the hallway—they're going to wonder why my room smells like a strawberry milkshake. If you get the air freshener and spray a bunch, we can just say we were trying out my new present." She gave him a lopsided grin. "You must be psychic."

Daniel frowned his confusion. "Why do you say that?"

"Because you knew exactly what to get me. Your intuition must have told you we'd be needing a strawberry-scented cover soon." Angel fell back on the bed giggling.

Daniel's frown turned into a scowl. "Well, something must have told me you'd scare the heck out of me and make me spill your milkshake."

"*My* milkshake? Don't you mean *your* spilled milkshake? Besides, you owe me after that mean birthday-gift-box trick. I was so excited to see what you got me and share it with my friends." She thrust out her lip in a fake semblance of a pout. "The least you could have done was buy some strawberry-scented perfume. Then I could have sprayed them all, and we'd all smell like strawberries!" She nodded toward the still-full cup, which Daniel had placed on her nightstand. "How about we share that remaining milkshake, Danny-Boy? Do you think that's fair?"

Daniel ignored her question for the moment and took the last of the soiled paper towels back into the bathroom. After washing his hands, he returned with the can of air freshener and sprayed the room, turning in a circle until he'd covered the entire area in the thin mist. He took a deep breath. The sweet smell cooled his ire a little. He then set the can on the table beside the bed, picked up his bookbag, and sank into the blue-vinyl chair. Finally, he looked at her and sighed.

"Angel, I'm really mad at you." He spoke softly yet forcefully, hoping to make her understand. "You scared me. You weren't moving, and I thought you were comatose or worse. I was just about to hit the emergency call button when you popped up like a jack-in-the-box!"

Apparently unfazed over being chastised, Angel giggled. "You should have seen the expression on your face, Daniel. You looked like you saw a ghost! I'm sorry for scaring you, but believe it or not, it was a good lesson for you."

"You were trying to teach me a lesson?" Daniel glared. "That's even worse."

"What do you mean?"

"I *mean*, little kids don't always think about how their jokes or pranks might affect other people. I figured you were just goofing around…trying to scare me without considering how I might feel. I thought you might be dead, Angel. That's not funny at all!" Daniel shook his head. "Lesson or no lesson, you shouldn't joke around about stuff like that."

Angel sat quietly for a moment, and Daniel could tell she was deep in thought. After a moment, she nodded. "You're right, and I'm really, really sorry. I guess if I wasn't supposed to die sometime soon, my little prank would have been a little funnier... I just didn't think it through, I guess."

"Obviously not." Daniel crossed his arms. He glanced down at the book bag on the floor at his feet, thinking about the other gifts it contained. At the moment, he wasn't feeling very happy or generous. "Apology accepted... but don't you ever do that to me again, okay?"

Angel nodded. "Scout's honor."

"You're not a Scout, but I'll take you at your word. So...I guess you might as well tell me about this latest lesson of yours."

"Well, when I was under the blanket and not moving, I'll bet your heart was racing, and I bet you felt charged up, too. Negative emotions like fear and anger can shock us—fill us with energy and make us feel alive. But the electric jolt we experience from negative emotions doesn't sustain our life-force energy." She leaned toward him. "Do you know what does sustain us, Danny-Boy?"

"Strawberry milkshakes?" he asked, purposely giving her a flippant answer. He still hadn't fully forgiven her for scaring him. "Too bad yours ended up all over the floor. I guess I'm the only one who will be feeling energized and happy tonight."

She glanced over at the milkshake then back at him. "Yes, that last milkshake would help sustain you—but only for tonight. Love is what sustains us for life! I would be happy to educate you further on the life-enhancing power of love." She looked back over at the milkshake then grinned. "But only if you're willing to share? I can even use my own straw if you are worried about my germs. Cancer is not contagious, you know, but love is!"

"I'd love to learn more about love," he told her, "but I'll be honest with you, kid...I'm still a little upset with you."

Angel leaned over and grabbed his hand. She gave a tug until he moved, getting up from the chair to sit beside her on the bed.

"Oh, Daniel, I am sorry. Truly. You deserve my sincere apology, but it's just as important for you to give me your sincere forgiveness. We all need to embrace forgiveness before we can embrace unconditional love." She squeezed his hand. "If you remember, we talked earlier about how important it is for people to learn to forgive themselves. That's the first step.

But then we also have to reach out and forgive others in our lives. You've acknowledged you need to forgive yourself for what happened when you had that accident." She looked at him closely. "Is there someone else in your life—someone besides me, of course—who you need to forgive?"

Daniel turned his head, trying to avoid her questioning gaze, but she put a small hand on his cheek and gently turned his face back toward hers.

"Daniel, we all have someone stuck in our thoughts and in our hearts... someone we need to forgive. It could be a family member, a friend, a co-worker, or someone who crashed into our lives. We might not feel they deserve our forgiveness, but forgiving them will free our minds and open our hearts to love."

Daniel sighed. "First of all, I do forgive you. Sincerely." He laughed softly. "I don't think I could ever stay mad at you for long. And even though that was a pretty mean and thoughtless prank, I know you have a beautiful heart. You also have a creepy way of seeing right inside my soul, because you're right; I do have someone I need to forgive." Once again, Daniel looked away, past Angel to stare at the blank wall as his father's image filled his mind.

"Well, then you've got to forgive that person."

She spoke in a matter-of-fact voice, as if she were telling him he should order a pizza for dinner tonight.

"It's not quite that easy," he told her. He could feel her questioning stare, but he refused to meet her gaze. "This particular person doesn't deserve my forgiveness. He's one of those cockroaches, and I'd rather squish him like a bug than have him in my life." Bitterness echoed in Daniel's tone, and his love switch had turned off the moment he'd thought of his old man.

"Daniel, if a particular person popped into your mind when you thought about forgiveness, then he needs to be forgiven. That doesn't mean you have to welcome him with open arms back into your life, but you do have to release the negative emotions that are associated with that person." Angel squeezed his hand again, harder this time. "Think about how you're feeling right this moment. Not good, right? *You're* hurting because of the bad thoughts and emotions you associate with this guy. You *have* to forgive him—for your sake as much as his." She paused and sighed. "Look, I know it's not easy, but if it's any consolation, the process becomes less difficult with practice. And if you can accept the philosophy that all behavior makes sense, you'll be much better off."

"All behavior makes sense?" Daniel scoffed. "C'mon, Angel. I find that hard to believe."

"Well, the behavior makes sense to the person who's doing whatever it is they're doing," she explained. "If someone has harmed you, then try to understand there was a reason they did what they did. This can be challenging, especially if the behavior or actions were serious and intentional in nature. I learned this stuff online, Danny-Boy, and it rang true for me." She nodded. "Bottom line—forgiveness is the most important ingredient in the recipe for happiness. Here's a quote I read that might help you understand the importance of forgiveness:

'To forgive is the highest, most beautiful form of love. In return, you will receive untold peace and happiness'. Robert Muller said that."

Deep inside, Daniel recognized the truth in Angel's words. All he had to do was think about how rotten he felt when he thought about his dad. If he never forgave his father, then Daniel would walk around feeling like crap every time the man's name came up or something happened to remind him of his dad's existence. "Okay, you're probably right. If I want to become a flashy firefly, then I have to forgive the cockroaches in my life. But, Angel, I'm still struggling to forgive *myself*, never mind trying to forgive my deadbeat dad."

""Whoa! That explains it." She nodded.

"Explains what?"

"No wonder you're struggling with forgiveness and to keep your love switch turned on. Our parents are supposed to help light us up at an early age by feeding us an abundance of unconditional love. If you were on the receiving end of some bad parenting, then you definitely need to learn how to forgive."

Daniel shook his head adamantly. "Not bad parenting. I just had a bad dad. He left when I was really young, and he abandoned me and my mom for a sleazy, bimbo bitch. At least, that's how my mom referred to his girlfriend when I overheard their screaming matches on the phone. The old man left town, and he never returned. He never sent my mom any support money, and the last time we heard from him was when I got sentenced after the accident. He blamed my mom for raising a delinquent teenager. Can you believe it?" Daniel's voice rose on a wave of anger. "That SOB tried to blame my *mom* for my mistake! My mom is amazing. She's very loving and caring, and she did the best she could, raising me on her own! Throughout that horrible ordeal, she was always there for me, supporting me after the accident, visiting me in prison, and helping me get my life back on track. She's my rock, and I would do anything for her. As far as I am concerned, my dad doesn't exist, and he definitely doesn't deserve my forgiveness or my love!" Daniel's shoulders slumped, and he hung his head, staring down at the floor between his feet. "Sorry, Angel, but this is a grown-up, family matter, and I don't expect you to understand."

"Maybe one day you will grow up and become a dad?"

Daniel's head snapped up. "What? I don't think I'm ready for a relationship, never mind having kids."

"You got something against kids? Because we are pretty cool you know. Besides, you seem to have done a pretty good job raising Sox."

"That's because Sox doesn't talk back, and she doesn't pull pranks on her loved ones."

Angel crossed her arms. "Pulling pranks can be considered an expression of love, you know. Maybe Sox doesn't love her daddy?"

Daniel choked back a laugh. Angel always knew how to lighten a serious topic with humor. But his mood quickly turned somber again when he thought about forgiving his father. How could he forgive someone who was supposed to love him but who had abandoned him instead?

Angel took his hand again. "Daniel?"

He looked up at her, the seriousness in her tone drawing his attention. "Let me ask you a question…"

He nodded, bracing himself for what she might say next.

"Should the little girl's mother forgive you?"

Daniel frowned "What do you mean? And what does that have to do with my deadbeat dad?"

"I think you know. The little girl who was killed in the accident…do you want her mother to forgive you?"

Daniel knew where she was going with her question, and he didn't want to answer her. "I don't know," he said, pulling his hand from hers. "I think it's time for me to go."

He started to get to his feet.

"No, Daniel, please, don't go yet. Trust me. This is important for your healing, and this is essential for our mission to help light up the world with love. Please…think about this for a minute, and be honest. Would it help you if the little girl's mother forgave you?"

"First of all, it's not my mission to help light up the world with love; it's yours. Remember, I'm just here visiting as part of my community service. The judge sent me here, Angel; I didn't come here of my own accord."

The room went quiet as the mood darkened. The playfulness had slipped away, and an uncomfortable awkwardness was settling in. Angel's question had touched a nerve for Daniel, filling him with self-loathing and depression. For the first time since their visits began, he had gone out of his way to be mean and ugly. What he'd just said made it sound as if he didn't want to be there, and he had reminded her that his visitations were part of his punishment. Tonight's visit had started out badly, with Angel upsetting him with her little trick of "playing dead," and now, the evening seemed destined to end the same way—with bad feelings between them. Daniel wanted to escape, to forget all about Angel and her attempts to save him. They sat there in silence, each waiting for the other to say or do something first.

"You can have it," Angel said. "My tummy was upset all day today, and I probably shouldn't add fuel to the fire. You remember the mess I made the last time that I erupted."

Daniel sighed. The idea that she'd give up her share of their milkshake as a peace offering made him feel about two inches tall. She really was an angel, and he was nothing but a great, big meanie. "That's very kind of you," he told her, giving her a little smile, "but if you get sick, we can always cover up the evidence with your sweet, strawberry-scented air freshener." He leaned close and put his arm around her shoulders. "I'm sorry for my cruel comments, and I'm glad the judge sent me here. I love our visits, and I love you."

"Aww, thank you, Danny-Boy. I didn't think you meant what you said, and I forgive you." She gave him a quick hug then pulled back. "I propose a truce. Let's share that milkshake and talk about fun stuff. Did you notice the new color streak in my hair?" She pointed at her wig. "It's part of the love rainbow, which I would be happy to share with you. But before we get into that colorful conversation, why don't you tell me about your techno past."

"I thought you wanted to talk about something fun?" Daniel laughed. "I'm pretty sure you'll find the story of my 'techno past' a bit boring."

Angel shook her head. "You never know, Daniel... You never know." She grabbed the milkshake off the table, took a sip, then leaned back against her pillows as if settling in to listen. "Go ahead. You talk, and I'll sip this delicious shake."

"Okay, well, I was a computer geek in my former life, and I worked for a large, digital-game-design company. I was considered one of their top game designers, and they called me Digital Dan, but that part of my life was quickly disconnected following the accident. I lost my job, and the judge banned me from using technology and accessing the Internet and social media sites. The technology ban seemed excessive, but I think he was trying to send a strong message to my generation about the dangers of texting and driving. I also think he was trying to protect me from the online backlash on social media sites. I heard rumors about people calling me names like, Dangerous Driving Dan, Death Texter, Dan, and even Kid Killer. I deserved to be punished through the justice system, but I didn't deserve to be persecuted by a bunch of online tormentors."

Angel gaped at him. "That's terrible, Daniel. You did *not* deserve to be bullied or threatened online like that! It's probably a good thing the judge sheltered you from the online attacks, but I'm sure your family and friends felt persecuted, too. I guess that's why my dad is so paranoid about me surfing the Internet. My mom keeps reassuring him that I have strict, iPad-use rules to follow, but I don't blame him for wanting to protect his little girl. It's too bad there are people out there who abuse and misuse the Internet in so many different ways. The cockroaches always seem to hang out in the dark corners of the world, including the vulnerable nesting sites online." She paused and giggled. "Maybe we need to hatch more fireflies online to help light up those dark corners. What do you think, Danny-Boy, could we use technology to help light up the world with love?"

Instead of answering her, he asked, "How many of those iPad-use rules have you broken lately?"

"I told you; I learned my lesson after the pizza-delivery fiasco, and I continue to use discretion while surfing online. How do you think I ended up with the beautiful love rainbow in my hair?" Once again, she stroked her long, colorful wig. "Do you like it? I have a few more colors to add before it is complete."

He shook his head, wondering who was better at changing the subject—him or her. "It looks beautiful, Angel, and it reminds me that you are a cool, colorful kid. Your insights and ideas are inspiring, and I agree we could use technology to help light up the world with love. There are a lot of great sites and social media channels that are spreading loving messages and promoting positive changes. Most of my industry experience was in developing online games for entertainment purposes—I suppose you could say our mission was to help gamify the world. So, yeah, there's an opportunity to help lovify the world using a digital-gaming platform. My ban from technology ends in two weeks, which coincides with the end of my eight weeks of community service. Now…hand over that milkshake, will you?"

Angel absently passed him the shake. "What are you saying?" she asked. "Are you trying to tell me we only have two weeks of visits left? What are your plans after that?" She leaned forward and grabbed his arm. "You're not going to abandon me, are you? What about my supply of strawberry milkshakes? You wouldn't dare deprive a very sick kid of her only pleasure in life, would you?"

Daniel laughed and patted her hand. "It's okay, kid. Relax. Weren't you listening before? I love you. I'd never abandon you. You'll still get your milkshakes. Which reminds me…" Daniel leaned down and grabbed his backpack off the floor. He reached inside and fished around until he found the colored pencils and little sketch pad he'd bought her. "I got these on my way to visit you today. I hope you'll be able to put them to good use."

He set the art supplies on the bed between them.

"Oh, Daniel! I love them!" Angel picked up the pad and leafed through the crisp, white, clean pages, and then she examined the box of colored pencils. "I love to draw, and I'm sure these will help pass many boring hours." She leaned forward and hugged him. "Thank you."

Daniel's cheeks grew warm as he returned her embrace, careful to hold the milkshake cup out of the way so it wouldn't spill. "You're welcome. Now…stop worrying. I promise I'll come visit you every Friday, no matter what."

Angel pulled back. She shook her head. "I can't believe it's been six weeks since you appeared in my life. You crawled into my room like a cockroach, but you have since sprouted wings like a firefly, and now, I think you're ready to light up with love. I really am grateful for our friendship, and I'm excited about the opportunity to work together on a mission to light up the world with love. I believe in synchronicities, and I feel that you and I were meant to connect for our personal healing and for global healing." She gave him a penetrating look. "If you're sincere about using your computer and online-gaming skills to help 'lovify the world', as you termed it, then I have one important question for you. *When can we start?*"

Daniel laughed and held up his free hand. "Whoa, slow down, Angel of love. I'm not even reconnected to technology yet, and as you know, I still have a lot of my own personal healing to do."

Angel leaned back against the pillows, closed her eyes, and drew several deep breaths. She looked paler than normal, and Daniel's concern for her grew. She rarely seemed as sick as she was, and sometimes, he forgot she had a terminal illness. How she managed to maintain such a positive attitude was beyond him. He waited patiently for her to respond to his last statement. Finally, she opened her eyes again and looked at him.

"I know, Daniel, and I don't mean to pressure you, but when you only have a short time to live, you want to fulfill your purpose before your time is up. I wonder how many people never get to fulfill their purpose. It's probably easier to live a safe life than to take a few risks and live a purposeful life. Does fear hold people back, or is it a lack of understanding of the purpose for their life? We all have a purpose in life, and we all share a collective purpose, too. Danny-Boy, you and I are supposed to work together on the collective purpose. Does that make sense to you?" She stopped and gave him a beseeching look. "You're not afraid, are you?"

He shook his head sadly. "No, I'm not afraid, and it does sort of make sense. But as I've already told you several times, I'm just not sure I'm ready."

"Daniel, I have to ask you an important question, but I don't want you to get mad at me or run out on me." She spoke softly, pausing now and then to breathe. "If the little girl's mother forgave you, would that make you feel better? I know it is unlikely that she would show up at your door and offer her forgiveness, but if you received a message of forgiveness, would that help you heal?"

"You're right; I'd rather run than think about the answer to that question, but since we're friends, I'm going to stay and do my best to explain how I feel." He figured if she had the strength for this conversation, the least he could do was try to find the strength to answer her. "First of all, I would never expect her to forgive me, and I wouldn't blame her if she never did, either. Hell, I made a terrible decision that resulted in the death of her daughter. Why should she forgive me?" Thinking about these things made his stomach ache, and he rubbed his abdomen absently in an effort to relieve the pain there.

"I know…it's tough to talk about this. But please try to think of it as a hypothetical question."

"How does a seven-year-old kid come up with such big words? Is Pinky giving you spelling and grammar lessons, too? By the way, no need to answer my rhetorical questions. In answer to your hypothetical one, yes, it would probably help me feel better if she forgave me. But that seems obvious, so why ask?"

She nodded. "Yes, it's obvious, but there's a second part to this question. Let's just say she forgave you; do you think *she* would feel better?" Angel paused, then added, "Oh, and by way, that's *not* a rhetorical question; I really want you to answer from your heart."

God…this kid. "I guess so. I'm sure it would be very difficult for her to forgive me, but I imagine she would feel a bit better, too. If she *really* forgave me, then she wouldn't have to deal with all those negative emotions she's got to be feeling toward me."

"Exactly!" Angel beamed, obviously pleased with his answer. "Forgiveness helps to heal the recipient and the person offering the forgiveness. In most cases, an apology isn't even required to prompt the forgiveness because the other person already knows you're sorry. For instance, before you apologized to me, I already knew you were sorry for the mean things you said earlier. Do you think the little girl's mother knows you're sorry for what happened?"

"Yes, I *know* she does. The judge gave me an opportunity to apologize in court, but I never did get to speak directly to the family outside of the courtroom. I hope they're aware of how sad I am and how sorry I am for what I did to cause them such an enormous loss." He paused, thinking back to his first few weeks in prison. "I even thought about writing a letter to them, but the judge ordered me not to have any contact with the victim's family. I think it was even written in the formal sentencing and probation conditions. To be honest, I would be afraid to see them, even if I was allowed to contact them."

Angel shook her head. "You don't have to see them. I'm about to share something else with you—something else I learned online. They refer to it as 'giving and receiving forgiveness using heart-centered visualization'." She smiled. "I know. Sounds crazy. And whenever possible, it's better to offer forgiveness in person, where people are face-to-face, eye-to-eye, and heart-to-heart. But sometimes, that's just not possible, either because of geographical distances, emotional separation, or, like in your case, legally imposed boundaries. Fortunately, we can use visualization to practice the art of forgiveness."

"Angel, this all sounds—"

"Wait," she interrupted him. "Before you say anything, Danny-Boy, this is not my medications talking. People have done a lot of research into this, and they've discovered that our thoughts and intentions are powerful communication links. We can contact someone intuitively, just by thinking about them. Have you ever had someone pop into your mind, or have you thought about calling someone and then the phone rings, or have you felt another person's feelings?"

Daniel'd had enough for one visit. The later it got, the loopier their conversations seemed to get. Time to cut out before she started talking about other dimensions and out-of-body experiences. "Yes, I have," he told her. "But right now, I'm thinking about the bus driver as he opens the door and lets me in so I can go home and go to sleep. Say good night, Angel."

"Wait, you can't go yet." She sat forward. "I didn't tell you about the love rainbow in my hair, and I know you were curious."

"Nice try, sweetie, but you've tried to keep me here with promises of divulging that information several times already." He got to his feet. "Besides, you admitted it wasn't complete yet, so I think I'll wait to hear about the love rainbow when it's all done. How about next week?"

She gave him her pouty face. "Okay, you're on to me. I admit I'm afraid of the dark, and when the flashy firefly leaves, I feel alone and scared. So please, stay for just a little longer, and I promise I'll send you home with a special gift. Besides, you don't want to make a sick little girl feel afraid and unhappy, do you?" She looked up at him and batted her eyelashes.

Daniel busted out laughing. "How can I possibly say no to you? Especially when you use guilt to get your way." He sat back down on the blue-vinyl chair. "I'll hang out for a little while longer, but I need to remind you that you can turn your love light on anytime you are afraid of the dark. Unless, of course, you are not really afraid of the dark?"

"Oh, so now the student wants to become the teacher. I hope you realize that angels are natural fireflies, and we can light up anytime we want. You can do the same, Daniel, but first, you need to clear out the dark patches on your heart."

"Should I be afraid of these supposed dark patches on my heart?"

"Good question. You know, most people are afraid of forgiveness because they're afraid of opening up their hearts and becoming vulnerable. That's probably why there are so many unresolved relationship issues with ex-spouses, isolated family members, long-lost friends, and broken business partnerships. Some people will choose to take their unresolved issues to their grave rather than trying to resolve them through the art of forgiveness." She paused and smiled. "Danny-Boy, I'm handing you a life-saving gift. If you learn the art of forgiveness, you'll be able to heal yourself and heal others. Forgiveness helps to remove those dark patches on our hearts. Whether you're asking for forgiveness or offering it, you can practice through visualization. All you have to do is hold a picture of the person in your mind, embrace them within a heart-shaped image, and then, depending on the issue, you can ask for their forgiveness or offer your forgiveness." Once again, she paused and grinned at him. "I know it seems a bit far out there, but the other person will receive your message, and both of you will receive what you need for healing. It works wonders, and the cool thing is that you can practice the art of forgiveness anywhere and anytime. Are you ready to give it a try?"

Daniel shrugged. As usual, he wished he could tell her what she wanted to hear, but he just couldn't. "I'm not sure; maybe it's best for me to sleep on this one."

"I realize it can be a difficult concept to grasp, but if you're willing to give it a try, I guarantee you'll experience some emotional healing the first time you try it. Your best bet is to pick the person who's weighing heaviest on your heart, but you can practice it with anyone. Are you willing to try it?" she asked yet again.

Daniel laughed. "Do I have a choice? I think you're probably going to keep bugging me until I give in?"

Angel giggled. "You know me well, Daniel, but I appreciate your openness and willingness to try. I'll walk you through the first one, and then you can practice on your own. Would it be okay if we tried asking the little girl's mother for forgiveness?"

Daniel shrugged. "Maybe we should start with someone else?" He sighed. "I really hate to disappoint you, Angel, but like I said before, I don't think I deserve her forgiveness."

Angel leaned forward and took his hand. "Daniel, we all deserve forgiveness, including you. Heck, *especially* you. After everything you've been through, you deserve forgiveness from others, and you need to forgive yourself. Close your eyes and hold an image of the little girl's mother in your mind, embrace her in a heart-shaped image, and then silently repeat these words." She looked at him closely. "Are you ready?"

He nodded reluctantly.

"Okay. Here it goes. Say to yourself, *I'm sorry, and I sincerely ask for her forgiveness.* Use your imagination, see your message being delivered, and have faith it will be received. Trust that you'll also receive the peace and happiness that comes with forgiveness." She sighed. "I know you think this is a little crazy, but you need to trust me. It takes practice, Danny-Boy, but like they say, practice makes perfect, so be persistent and patient."

Wanting to reassure her, Daniel took her hand and gave it a squeeze. "Thank you, Angel. Really. I know you mean well, and I'll do the best I can."

Angel held his gaze. "I hope you understand how important this step is for your healing and for the healing of others. You can use this visualization technique to ask for forgiveness and to offer your forgiveness." She paused, then asked quietly, "Do you think you could try forgiving your dad using this method?"

No. Maybe. I don't know... Daniel sighed. "Angel, I don't know what to say or even what to think right now. I never expected to be talking about my deadbeat dad, and I *definitely* never considered forgiving him."

Angel squeezed his hand. "Please, don't be mad at me, Daniel. I know this is an emotional and sensitive issue for you. You have to trust me, though. I know in *my* heart that practicing the art of forgiveness with your dad will help you heal *your* heart." She giggled and gave him a lopsided grin. "You don't need to say anything else, but before you can say goodnight for the last time tonight, I have a fun suggestion. Well…fun and maybe a little nuts. I've come up with a way we can help remind each other to keep our love switch turned on. Instead of saying good-bye or goodnight, let's say, 'Love on'." Again, she giggled, every bit the seven-year-old little girl. "What do think, Danny-Boy, wouldn't that be fun?"

Daniel couldn't bring himself to answer her right away. His first reaction was to laugh at such a ludicrous suggestion. Love on? Really? "I mean, maybe we could say that to each other privately, but—"

"Oh, I see; you're worried about what other people might think of you." She smiled and shook her head. "You really need to get over that. But for now, how about if I say it? You can say it back when you don't feel so embarrassed." "Love on, Danny-Boy." She yawned. "And now, I'm going to bed. I'm exhausted. Goodnight, and please make sure you take the empty cups with you. And maybe grab the trash bag out of the bathroom and take it with you?" She nodded toward the restroom. "We don't want the mess you made to get you into any more trouble."

The mess I made…? Daniel shook his head.

He retrieved the empty milkshake cup from the nightstand, took it into the bathroom, and added it to the trash with the milkshake-soiled paper towels. He tied the bag and carried it back into the bedroom.

"Goodnight, Angel, sleep tight, and don't let your Love On bite." He left the room, trash bag slung over his shoulder.

"That was lame, Daniel, very lame," she called out after him.

*****

As Daniel exited the back door of the hospice, he couldn't stop himself from laughing. He loved teasing his little Angel, especially during his dashing exits. Tonight's visit was longer than his previous ones, and he had to hurry to catch the bus home. Not that he really minded. He didn't want to stand around too long at the bus stop anyway. Angel had pushed a sensitive, childhood-memory button that had triggered a flow of mixed emotions for Daniel. He had buried his father in the back of his mind, but the troubling thought of forgiving his dad brought the man back to life in Daniel's consciousness. He made it to the bus stop just in time. As he boarded the bus, he tried to avoid eye contact with the other passengers and was relieved to find an empty seat at the back. He slumped down, lowered his head, and closed his eyes in an effort to shut out the painful memories. He'd done his best to hide his conflicted emotions from Angel, but now that she couldn't see his reaction, he allowed the pain to rise to the surface.

Although he despised his father for abandoning him and his mother, he'd spent most of his childhood secretly waiting for him to appear at special times of the year. On his fifth birthday, Daniel had refused to open his gifts. "Not until Daddy gets here," he'd said. His mother had gently cradled him to sleep as she reassured him that everything would be okay. The more he thought about the sacrifices his mother had endured, the more he loved her and the more he hated his dad. As he sat on the lonely bus seat, he struggled with the thought of forgiving his father. Angel's words kept echoing in his mind. *Practicing the art of forgiveness with your dad will help you heal your heart.*

Emotional exhaustion was making Daniel feel vulnerable. In a desperate attempt to get some relief, he closed his eyes and dragged a blurry image of his dad out of his memory bank and into the present moment. Confusion, disappointment, anger, sorrow, pity, and guilt flooded his thoughts. Angel's guidance directed him to embrace his father in a heart-shaped image. Daniel could clearly see his father captured in a heart-shaped picture frame. He took a deep breath, and he silently delivered a heart-felt message. *Dad, I don't understand why you left us, but I forgive you.*

The sounds of someone sobbing brought Daniel's attention back to the bus. He looked up, realizing his cheeks were wet with tears, and he had been the one crying. *God, how embarrassing.* He glanced across the aisle. An older lady seated a few rows away stared back at him with compassion in her eyes. She couldn't know why he was crying, but he saw understanding in her steady gaze. Daniel looked down and dried away his tears with the sleeve of his jacket.

The rest of the bus ride home felt like an emotional rollercoaster, and when they finally reached his stop, he breathed a sigh of relief. He exited the bus and walked down the block to his basement apartment. He slipped quietly through the door, dropped his bag in the dark foyer, and took refuge in the comfort of his bed. He didn't even bother brushing his teeth or checking his messages. His mother usually left a voice message on his answering machine, asking how his Friday-night visit had gone, but Daniel was in no mood for sharing. All he wanted to do was lose himself in sleep and forget about his swirling, conflicted thoughts. He pulled his thick blanket up in a feeble attempt to cover up the emotional wound that had been exposed.

"Come on, Dad, just one more pitch. I know I can hit this one out of the yard."

"We have to go in and wash up for dinner, Son."

Daniel's mom had yelled for them to come inside twice already, and the next time she had to call for them, they'd both most likely be in deep trouble. But Daniel wanted just one more chance to hit a home run...

"We can pretend we didn't hear her," Daniel said. "Besides, she's not going to ground both of us."

"Okay, one more pitch, but then that's it." His dad palmed the baseball. "I won't get grounded, but I might end up sleeping in the doghouse tonight."

Daniel giggled. "Buster would never let you in his doghouse, Dad. Don't you know, that's where he hides all of Mom's missing shoes?"

"So that's where they've all disappeared to! I thought that crazy dog was burying them in the field." His dad laughed and got into position to throw another pitch. "Okay, now we have to finish up so I can retrieve what's left of Mom's shoes. One of these days, she's going to catch that dog in the act, and then he's going to be minced meat!"

Daniel held the bat and bent his knees a little, just like his dad had showed him. His gaze never left the ball. "Mom loves Buster," he said. "She'd never hurt him." He raised the bat a little. "Okay, I'm ready. Make it a good one."

His dad let loose a perfect pitch, and Daniel watched the ball fly toward him through the air. He waited until the right moment then swung with all his might. The bat and ball collided with a loud crack, and the ball sailed through the air, up and over the fence into Mr. Martin's garden.

"Wow! Holy macaroni!" his dad shouted. "What a hit!"

Daniel tossed the bat onto the ground and ran to his dad. His father opened his arms, and Daniel jumped into his father's embrace.

"That was really great, Son," his dad whispered against his hair and hugged him tightly. "Way to go, Slugger!"

Daniel woke up in a pool of sweat, his cheeks wet with tears he'd cried in his sleep. The blanket twisted around his legs and torso felt like it was squeezing the life out of his tired body. He had to wiggle free of its embrace before he could sit up and take a deep breath. He'd tossed and turned most of the night, and now, as he sat in bed in the predawn darkness, he tried to wrap his mind around the disturbing dream. Why was he suddenly having dreams about playing baseball with his dad? The old man had left when Daniel was only five years old, shortly after that day they'd played ball in the front yard, and Daniel had hit it "out of the park" and into their neighbor's garden. For the most part, Daniel had been deprived of any fun, father/son, childhood memories. He knew there had to be some—his dad had been there for the first five years of Daniel's life, and when he was around, they did things together. But once his father had left, nightmares had set in, disturbing Daniel's sleep for almost an entire year. Daniel shivered as he recalled the details of those terrifying dreams. He was just a little kid—maybe five or six years old—and almost every night, he would dream of his dad. While Daniel could see his father, a glass wall stood between them. At first, his dad would smile and wave, but then flames would ignite all around his father's body, and his father would scream and cry out for help. Daniel would reach out, pound on the glass in an attempt to break through, but he could never touch his dad or pull his father to safety. Every day during that first year after his dad had abandoned them, Daniel's mother would often rush into his room in the middle of the night to comfort him as he shivered with fear and sobbed, heartbroken over his father's absence.

*****

Daniel made his way through the rest of that day in a zombie-like state. He tried to clear his head by going for a walk, but he kept reliving last night's disturbing dream. As he re-entered his apartment, the flashing light on his answering machine caught his attention. Not many people had his number, and his mom usually called on Saturday mornings just to chat and on Wednesday afternoons to confirm their dinner plans for Thursday. This being a Saturday, he figured at least one of the messages must be from her, but who had left the other one?

He pressed the button and stood there, listening as his mother's voice filled the room.

"Daniel, call me as soon as you get home. I love you, honey."

Daniel deleted that message; the machine beeped twice and then began to play the second message.

"Daniel, honey, you need to call me tonight; it's important," his mother said.

Although he wasn't feeling up to talking to his mom, her messages had stoked his curiosity. She hadn't sounded frantic, but he knew her well enough to recognize the note of concern and maybe even a little bit of surprise in her tone. He picked up the phone and dialed her number.

"Hi, Mom," he said.

"You sound sad," she said. "Is everything okay? Has something happened with Angel? Did something happen at work yesterday?"

"No, nothing happened," he told her, forcing himself to sound happier than he felt just then. "Angel's fine, as far as I know, and work is work… Boring, but at least I'm paying all my own bills."

"Well, you don't sound so good. Maybe you're coming down with something. When we get off the phone, I want you to make yourself a cup of tea with honey and lemon, and get some rest. The last thing you need is to get sick right now."

Daniel smiled at her mothering advice. He'd be in his fifties, and if Mom was still around, she'd still be treating him as if he were a little kid.

"Okay. I'll do that. I promise. Now...why did you call? Sounded like you had something important to tell me?" he asked, holding the phone between his ear and his shoulder so he could fill the teapot.

"Yes, I do have something to tell you. You're not going to believe this..." She hesitated, drew a deep breath, then went on. "Your dad called today, and he wants to see you."

Daniel fumbled with the teapot, water sloshed all over the front of his shirt, and the phone slipped from his shoulder and dropped to the floor. "Shit."

He quickly set the teapot onto the counter and retrieved the phone.

"Mom? Sorry. You still there?" Daniel asked. His mind raced. His dad had called? How crazy was that? The night before, Daniel had dreamed about his father, and now, after all these years, out of the blue, the old man was calling and asking to see him?

"I'm here. Are you okay? What happened?"

His mother's concern sounded in her voice, and rather than add to her worry by telling her about his emotional meltdown on the bus or the strange dream, he decided to make light of the situation.

"Oh, um, I was trying to talk to you and fill the teapot at the same time, and I accidentally dropped the phone." He forced a laugh as he brushed at the water that had splashed all down the front of his t-shirt. "Guess I'm a bit of a klutz."

"Hmm. Okay, if you say so," she said. "Well, what about your father? Will you see him?"

Daniel shook his head. "No. I can't— I don't want to see him right now, Mom." He paused and thought about the situation for a moment, before adding, "Maybe we could talk on the phone or something?"

"All right... Daniel, I—" She stopped speaking and drew in a deep breath. "Never mind. We can talk about this some other time. I'll let you go finish making your tea. Get some rest, okay, dear?"

"Yes, Mommy," Daniel said, smiling. "Thanks for letting me know about the phone call. I'll talk to you again on Wednesday."

As Daniel ended the call and put the phone back on the charger on the kitchen counter, he couldn't help but think about his visit with Angel the night before. Was there a connection between the forgiveness visualization and the unexpected contact from his dad? As strange as it seemed, he trusted Angel and her weird ideas. He was willing to try to forgive his father from a distance, but Daniel had no desire to see his old man. And what else had his mother wanted to tell him? He suspected she'd had more she wanted to reveal, but he was too tired to think about all that right now. He had to trust the answers would be revealed at the right time...

WEEK 7

Friday night could not arrive soon enough for Daniel. He had been practicing "the art of forgiveness" technique all week, and he was excited to share his experiences with his little Angel. He was getting better at visualization, and he was striving to picture the facial expressions of the people he mentally placed in heart-shaped frames. He struggled to recall what his father looked like—after all, it had been something like sixteen years since Daniel had last seen the man. Recalling the face of the little girl's mother was a lot easier; Daniel didn't think he'd ever forget the woman's expression, her cheeks wet with tears, as she'd ran to the scene of the accident that day. The image made his chest ache, and when he mentally sent her messages, telling her how sorry he was and asking for her forgiveness, her expression appeared strained, as if she were having a difficult time with his request. He could only hope and pray this visualization technique would offer some comfort and healing for her, because something was *definitely* changing within Daniel's heart.

That Wednesday evening, he was sitting on his lumpy couch, practicing the forgiveness technique. After he'd sent messages to his father and the little girl's mom, Daniel had an idea. What if he tried the same thing with his ex-girlfriend Elizabeth? He had no trouble picturing Beth's pretty face embraced within a heart; however, sending messages asking for her forgiveness was a little more difficult. Her parents had rushed her off to college following the accident, and Daniel didn't know how she felt about anything that had happened. Did she hate him as much as her parents probably did? He'd lost all contact with her after she'd moved away, and he never expected to reconnect with her. But the quote Angel had shared with him had given him a sliver of hope.

If you love someone, set them free, and if they return, then it was meant to be.

The thought of reconnecting with Beth was all the encouragement he needed to give the art of forgiveness a try. If she forgave him, she might be willing to accept an invitation to meet up. But no matter what happened, at the very least, Daniel wanted her to know how very sorry he was for destroying their relationship. He could only imagine how badly she'd suffered due to his mistake.

*****

Two nights later, Daniel arrived at the hospice more excited to see Angel than ever. He was relieved to stroll past a quiet nurses' station because he felt guilty about sneaking in the special, Friday-night treats. This time, he'd also stopped at a little booth downtown earlier in the week and had purchased her a pretty little bracelet made of ceramic butterflies and beads. He couldn't wait to see the dainty piece of jewelry on her wrist.

Daniel was always nervous about the possibility that he might be questioned regarding the contents in his gym bag. Last week's milkshake disaster could have resulted in him having to make a confession. He wasn't sure how he would have explained the strawberry mess on the floor and the half-empty milkshake container in his bag. This week, as he entered Angel's room, he carefully set the gym bag on the table near the door before he approached Angel's bed.

The lights were off, the room was silent, and there were no visible signs of movement under the covers. Daniel frowned. Surely, she wouldn't try the same trick twice? Especially after he'd told her how frightened he'd been. Still, he approached the bed with caution, expecting her to jump up at any moment.

But as he neared the bed, a wave of concern washed over him. He had a bad feeling Angel was really sick this time. The shallow rise and fall of the blanket reassured him a little, but her being asleep in bed like this still wasn't a good sign. Normally, she'd be sitting up, watching TV or playing on her iPad, waiting for him to arrive.

In the light shining from the half-open bathroom door, he could see the top of her head, and his heart sank a little. Angel wasn't wearing her wig, and she looked so sick and so pale. A shadow of her normal self...

All these weeks, for the most part, he'd managed to avoid the fact that his little, loving friend was terminally ill and would die someday soon. The sight of her now was like a slap in the face, and tears filled his eyes and ran down his cheeks. He reached out and carefully, gently massaged her back. She was so thin, and he could feel nearly every bone in her spine.

God, he loved this kid. She was more than a good friend; she was like the little sister he'd never had. What would he ever do without her?

"Ahh, Danny-Boy, that feels so good." Angel shifted just a little on the bed. "My body is really achy today."

"Oh, Angel, I'm so sorry. You seem really sick tonight. Is there anything I can do to help?" He wished with all his heart that he could take away her pain.

"I'm not doing too good tonight. The nurses increased my medication this week. They said it would help me deal with the pain, but it makes me so sleepy. If you could continue rubbing my back, I would love that. I can feel the warmth of your hand. You are a good healer and a good friend, Danny-Boy, and I am so glad you came to visit me."

She spoke so softly, Daniel had to lean down to hear her.

"I wouldn't miss our Friday-night visits for anything." Daniel continued his gentle massage. "Guess what I have in my gym bag for us?" he said, hoping to make her happy.

"Oh, Daniel, you are such a sweetheart. I'm sorry, but I don't think I can drink anything—not even a milkshake—tonight. My tummy is too upset."

"That's okay." Gingerly, so as not to shake her, he lowered himself to sit on the edge of the bed. "We can save them, and maybe you'll feel a little better later." He searched his mind for something to talk about—something that might brighten her mood. "Do you want to hear about my practice this week with the art of forgiveness? I'm not sure how you did it, but your persistence to get me to try it paid off, big time."

Angel rolled over onto her back and looked up at him. "I'm really proud of you for being open and caring enough to help heal yourself and others. Practicing the art of forgiveness is like tending to a garden. You have to pull out the weeds to make room for the flowers to grow. Our guilt, shame, anger, and disappointment are like the weeds in our minds and in our hearts. When we practice the art of forgiveness, we are pulling out the weeds and making room for the love flowers to grow!"

"Wow." Daniel laughed. "Now you're talking like a flower child. They must have *really* increased your medication this week."

Angel giggled. "I'd rather be called a flower child than a weed man, Danny-Boy."

He took her hand, happy to see her smiling again and looking a little less pale. "What exactly are we lighting up the world with, Angel?"

"Love, Daniel, we are lighting up the world with love. It raises our frequency and gives us a natural high. So, Weedman, tell me all about your forgiveness trip this week. I'll remain silent if you can chat and rub my back at the same time."

"Sure," he said, "Roll over again, and I'll rub and talk."

He shifted a little closer, and for the next thirty minutes, he told Angel all about his experiences with forgiveness visualization. He talked about how difficult it had been to bring forth an image of his father's face, and how sad and uncomfortable the little girl's mother had appeared. He even told Angel about the dream he'd had—and the phone call from his father the next morning—and he admitted he'd tried the visualization technique with Beth.

"Who's Beth?" Angel asked, interrupting him for the first time since he'd begun speaking.

"Oh, that's right." Daniel laughed. "I never did tell you her name. Elizabeth Williams—Beth—was my girlfriend. I figured since I was apologizing to everyone else, I might as well let her know how sorry I am, too."

"I think that was a great idea," Angel mumbled into her pillow. "And that thing with your dad calling you? How awesome is that?"

Daniel sighed. "You know, I didn't take you too seriously last week. I had a hard time accepting and understanding your views on the art of forgiveness. But on the bus ride home, I thought about forgiving my dad. All at once, something opened inside me, and I became an emotional train wreck at the back of the bus. That same night, I had that crazy dream, where I was a little boy playing baseball with my dad." His throat grew tight, and he blinked hard to hold back the tears threatening to fall. "I woke up in a pool of tears. I felt a sense of longing, but I'm not sure if it was because

I was missing my dad or because I've lost all my good childhood memories. I don't remember having a fun, father/son relationship."

Angel sniffled, her nose buried in her pillow.

"Hey, kid, are you okay? Are you crying, sweetie? I didn't mean to upset you." He patted her shoulder. The last thing he wanted to do was make her feel worse than she already did tonight.

"Daniel," she murmured, turning her head and meeting his gaze, "I'm going to miss my dad. I love him so much. I'm his little princess, and he won't be able to see me grow up, and I can't tell you how sad that makes me. I'm afraid for him, too, because I don't know how he's going to handle it when I...when the day comes. He tries not to show how sad he is, but I've heard him crying out in the hallway." Angel's voice broke on a sob. She sucked in a deep breath, and her lower lip trembled. "My dad has always been the strong, silent one. He still doesn't talk much, but I know he's become softer, and I love my sweet, soft daddy."

Daniel's shoulders shook as he cried, and tears rolled down his cheeks. He could barely speak past the lump in his throat. "Angel, you have to be the kindest, most thoughtful, selfless person I've ever met. You're the one who is ill, and yet, your concern is always for others. I don't think I've ever seen you whine or feel sorry for yourself. Your strength amazes me. I wish I could be half as courageous as you are." He wiped his eyes with his sleeve and laughed self-consciously. "Sorry... I-I don't usually cry like this."

Angel reached for his hand. "It's okay to cry. Even big, tough men should be strong in spirit but soft in their emotions—that's what makes a real man, Daniel. And you're becoming a strong, kind, loving man. It sounds like you are making great progress practicing the art of forgiveness. But if you're thinking about your dad, it means you have unfinished love business to settle. And since he called, I'm guessing he's thinking about you, too. I don't believe in coincidences, but I do believe in the power of the forgiveness visualization. *I think* your dad got the message you sent him, and now he's reaching out."

Secretly, Daniel had thought the same thing, but he hadn't the courage to say it out loud. If what she was saying was true, and his dad had somehow "heard" Daniel's telepathic-like messages, did that mean the other people he'd apologized to—the little girl's mother and Beth—had heard the messages he sent their way, too? The thought both frightened and excited him.

"What are you thinking about, Danny-Boy? You're very quiet all of the sudden." Angel flipped back over and sat up, resting her arms on her knees. She cocked her head and grinned at him.

"Stop trying to read my mind, brat," Daniel said and then laughed. "I was just considering the possibility that you might be right. Maybe my dad did somehow sense I'd reached out to him, just not physically."

Angel giggled. "I would never try to read your mind. Who knows what kind of odd-ball thoughts I'd encounter in there!"

"Hmmph." Daniel shook his head at her jibe. "I see you're feeling a bit better." He got up off the bed to retrieve his backpack. "I don't know about you, but all that back-rubbing made me mighty thirsty."

"Hey, I'm only teasing you, Weedman. This flower child has all kinds of crazy thoughts, and you've heard most of them." She grinned. "And yes, thanks to you and your magical hands, I'm feeling a lot better. I was aching so badly when you came in; I didn't even want to move my eyelids." She eyed his backpack. "I think you read my mind. Is it strawberry-milkshake time?"

Daniel sank down onto the blue-vinyl chair, which, by this point, he figured had to have the indented imprint of his butt cheeks, and shook his head. "Nope."

Angel gave him her pouty face. "Nope? Why not?"

Daniel unzipped the outer pocket and retrieved the little, gift-wrapped box. "Because first, I have another present for you. When I saw it, I knew I had to get it for you." He held out the box and waited for her to take it.

"Another present? For me?" Angel squealed, obviously surprised and delighted, just as any other seven-year-old little girl would be. She started to reach for the box but then stopped and shook her head. "Before I open your gift, will you please pass me my wig? I always feel better when I'm wearing it, and it's looking so pretty now with all the different colors."

Daniel got to his feet and grabbed her wig from a hook on the wall on the other side of her nightstand. "Here you go."

He waited while she put it on, admiring the various strips of colors she'd added. She really had created a rainbow.

"*You* look pretty," he told her. "That wig wouldn't look nearly as nice on anyone else."

"Thanks, Daniel. My dad always tells me that bald is beautiful, but I prefer wearing my pretty, colorful wig. It makes me feel special, and it helps keep my head warm, too." She held out her hand and smiled. "Now I'm ready to open my present."

He gave her the box and sat watching while she carefully removed the wrapping paper, folded it, and set it aside. He shook his head at how precisely she slit each piece of tape holding the little box closed, but the look on her face when she finally opened the lid and pulled out her present was worth the wait.

"Oh, Daniel," she said, her voice laced with awe, "it's beautiful."

She held up the dainty bracelet, and the crystal beads separating the butterflies glittered in the light.

"Here, let me help you put it on," he told her.

She handed him the bracelet, and he unhooked the little clasp, wrapped the bracelet around her thin wrist, then refastened the closure.

"There," he said, sitting back to admire how pretty she looked…and how happy. His heart filled with joy at the sight of her smile.

"Thank you, thank you, thank you!" she cried. She fingered the tiny, colorful butterflies. "They are so sweet, and I'll wear this for the rest of my life!"

Daniel slumped down in his chair. "Angel…"

She looked up at him, her face beaming, and he shook his head.

"Never mind," he said. Obviously, she didn't realize what she'd just said or how her words had affected him. He dug back down inside the main compartment of his backpack and pulled out two milkshake containers. "Let's drink these before they completely melt away."

"Great idea!"

Daniel handed her a shake and then helped her get propped up leaning back on a stack of pillows. Once they were both settled and drinking their shakes, Angel smiled at him.

"I really do think it's awesome that your dad called you."

"Awesome?" Daniel smirked. "I'd call it ironic and a little weird that he wants to see me."

"It's not ironic, Daniel. It is synchronistic, and it's not surprising that he wants to see you. Our thoughts become powerful communication links when we practice the art of forgiveness. You have to trust that it's working, and healing is occurring for both you and your dad. The dark patches on your heart will disappear as your forgiveness removes the negative feelings and emotions."

"It sounds good in theory, Angel, but I don't have any desire to see my dad. I just want to forget about him, and move on in my life. If the art of forgiveness will help me release him, then I will definitely keep practicing." Just thinking about the possibility of having to see his father made Daniel's chest hurt.

"You know what they say...practice makes perfect, except when it comes to practical jokes. Isn't that right, Danny-Boy?" Angel winked.

"Most definitely. And from now on, I think you and I should forget about playing practical jokes on each other. If we don't, one of us is likely to get in trouble." He paused, and then carefully keeping a straight face, he asked, "Shall we shake on it?"

It took a moment for Angel to get the milkshake reference in his comment. But when she realized what he'd said, she let out a loud belly laugh that triggered a similar reaction in Daniel. If laughter was the best medicine, then they were both getting a healthy dose of humorous healing. Maybe that was what Angel's doctor would have prescribed for helping her cope with the cancer treatments. And maybe that's what the judge would have recommended for Daniel's rehabilitation. But Daniel didn't believe *anyone* could have known how significant his and Angel's friendship would become. They were bonding with love, laughter, and respect for each other. They were uncovering their destiny, and if Angel was correct—and Daniel had a feeling she was—they were launching a love mission that would help change the world.

"Daniel, have you ever thought about your own mortality?" Angel asked, suddenly sobering. "Have you thought about what others would say at your memorial?"

"I bet you're dying to know, aren't you?" he quipped, tongue in cheek.

"Not funny, Daniel," she said, giving him a mock glare. "Because as you know, I *am* dying." She shrugged. "But then again, so are you, and so is everyone else in the world. Are you afraid of death, Danny-Boy?"

Daniel looked away. "How did we get on this topic? I don't like to talk about death, Angel, especially since my negligent actions caused the death of a child. You know how guilty I feel."

"I know how guilty you felt when I first met you, and I know how much progress you've made around forgiveness. The dream about your dad was your wake-up call. The phone call from your dad was your confirmation that you have the power to practice and master the art of forgiveness. You mentioned that you want to release your dad, and I want to help you understand what that means. It is impossible to remove the person from our lives. They will always be an unexpected phone call or a text or an email or an unplanned visit or a passing thought—or an appearance in our dreams—away. Even if they pass away, our memories of them will live on. We can, however, remove the negative emotion or feeling that is associated with that person. There might be others in your life that you want to release, too, so I would like to share the forgiveness visualization with you from a higher perspective."

Daniel closed his eyes for a moment and drew in a deep breath. Was he ready to hear more of Angel's views on life and love? So far, she hadn't led him wrong, but was he prepared to take the next step in this journey? He met her steady gaze. "Okay, Flower Power Child, how high do I have to get to understand this one?"

"Oh, Mr. Weedman, why do you have to sound so worried all the time? For this visualization, all you are going to need is a good imagination and some Angel wings. Are you ready to fly high with me?"

"Does your mother know you're experimenting with medicinal herbs?" he joked, still trying to delay getting into a deeper conversation.

"Trust me," she said, her expression serious, "I'm naturally high on love, and I want to help raise you up, too. If we're going to work together to help light up the world with love, then we need to see things from a higher perspective. We need to start our flight from the end point in our lives. My dad always says there are only two certain things in life—death and taxes. Since I'm too young to pay taxes, I would like to share some valuable insights on death, forgiveness, and love. Consider what I'm about to share with you as your reward for spending so much time visiting a sick kid."

Daniel's cheeks grew warm, and he felt as if he had a band tightening around his chest. "Angel, our visits are priceless, and I don't think the judge calculated how much value I would receive from our time together. Next Friday will be eight weeks, and the time has really flown by."

"Eight weeks. Right. So you said before. Your time is almost up. So, after next Friday, how can I guarantee you'll come back to see me?" she asked him. "There won't be anything stopping you from staying home and watching movies all night every weekend."

"I told you there's nothing to worry about. I enjoy our visits."

"Still… I wonder what would happen if you violated any of the conditions of your probation? Would you get sentenced to some additional community service time? Maybe I would get to see you for another eight weeks?"

She moved her hand over toward the nurses' call buttons. There were two of them—one for emergency response and one for non-emergency response.

Daniel narrowed his eyes at her. "Angel, what do you think you're doing?"

"I think I need a little insurance that you'll continue with our Friday-night visits, Danny-Boy."

Her intentions became clear in an instant. If she pressed one of those buttons, a nurse would come running, and they'd both get caught with the strawberry-milkshake contraband Daniel had snuck in. And while Angel might get scolded, Daniel would most likely get into much deeper trouble.

"Angel, don't you dare—"

Her hand came down on the non-emergency call button before he could complete his sentence. For a moment, they stared at each other, Angel smirking and Daniel too shocked to move.

"Someone will be here any second," she told him smugly.

Her words sent him into a flurry of action, and he scrambled to snatch up the milkshake cups and shove them into his backpack. He'd no sooner closed the zipper then the nurse came rushing into the room.

"What's going on in here? Is something wrong?" the nurse asked.

Daniel didn't turn around. Instead, he stared at Angel, waiting for her to respond.

"Well?" the nurse asked, her impatience evident in the tone of her voice. "One of you hit the call button. What do you need?"

Daniel looked from Angel's smug expression, back over his shoulder at the nurse. The poor woman looked harried and worn out, and Daniel felt sorry for her. Still, Angel had a lesson coming to her for breaking their truce.

"Thank you for coming so quickly," he told the nurse. "Angel is probably too embarrassed to say anything, but a little bit ago, she said she thought she saw a cockroach run under her bed."

There, he thought... *let's see her get herself out of this one.*

He looked back at Angel, delighted to see she had the good grace to look worried.

"A cockroach!" The nurse addressed Angel. "Are you certain? We've never had any bugs around here that I know of. Are you sure you weren't hallucinating? Sometimes, the medication you're taking can make patients see things that aren't really there."

Angel finally pulled herself together enough to speak. "I'm sure you're probably right. I mean, I was really groggy when I woke up, and I did think I saw some kind of bug crawling around down there"—she nodded toward the floor beside her bed—"but I haven't seen anything since, so..."

Angel glared at Daniel as her words trailed off, and he grinned back at her. No doubt, she'd considered what might happen if she'd insisted she'd seen a cockroach. The nurse would have to file an official complaint, and chaos would reign as exterminators came in to search for bugs and possibly even fumigate the whole place.

"Well," the nurse said, hands on her hips, "let me know if you see anything else. Meanwhile, I have medications to administer and other patients to tend to."

"Yes, ma'am," Angel murmured, "I'm sorry to have bothered you."

"Thank you again," Daniel said politely. "I'll keep an eye on Angel, just in case she starts seeing things again..."

The nurse huffed, gave them both a stern glare, and then retreated hastily from the room, leaving Daniel chuckling softly at having put his bratty little Angel in her place.

"I hope you're proud of yourself, Danny-Boy. The nurses are going to think I'm crazy, and they might even increase my medication to help calm my nerves."

Daniel laughed. "Don't worry, Angel, I'm sure they already know you're a bit crazy." He gave her a pointed look. "So, should we call another truce?"

"If you think I'm crazy now, just wait until we take our first Angel flight together. Rather than shake hands on the ground, I think it would be more appropriate if we fluttered our feathers together high up in the sky. That would be like ratifying our truce in Heaven; then we would have to stick to it."

The way she phrased the suggestion was as colorful as the wig she wore, but Daniel wasn't buying her contrition for a minute. "For some reason, I don't think you have the willpower or the desire to end our little game. But I'm willing to fly with you, Angel, as long as we're back in time for breakfast."

"It's nice to know you still trust me, and I promise you'll be back long before breakfast. In fact, I'll have you back in time for some sweet dreams tonight. So get comfortable, and I'll help guide you along on our flight."

Daniel sighed and settled back in the chair, wondering what to expect from her next. He did trust her, had put his heart in her little hands, and now he had to trust her enough to believe she could help him take his healing to the next level. She loved to joke around, but what they were doing now was serious business.

"If you're ready," she said, interrupting his musings, "close your eyes, open your mind, and soften your heart. Picture yourself at your own memorial, and see your loved ones in attendance. Take your time, and try to see the expressions on their faces as they pay their last respects to you. You might see them shedding tears or hanging their heads in sorrow or wishing they had one more moment with you. Try to feel their love and their emotions. What would your family and friends be saying about you? How would you like to be remembered? Would you have any regrets or unfinished love business? If you could go back into your life, what would you say to those in attendance? Would you tell them you loved them? Would you apologize to the ones you harmed? Would you forgive those who harmed you? Remember, forgiveness is the key to unlock the unconditional love in ourselves and in the lives of others.

"While it's important to make peace with the loved ones who are close to you, it's just as important to make peace with those who crossed your path throughout your lifetime. This part of the visualization involves seeing your life from a higher perspective. Keep your eyes closed, strap on your high-vision glasses, and prepare to take flight. Rise up slowly, and look down at the crowd of people at your memorial. Send thoughts of comfort to your loved ones, and know your loving thoughts will help ease their sorrow and sadness. Doing this will also help release you so you can continue spiraling up to a higher vantage point.

"You can imagine you have the wings of an angel, or, if you prefer, you can use drone technology and your imagination to help you hover over your life. The higher you rise, the more people you will encounter from your past. You might have only had a brief encounter or a distant contact with them. You might have to scan your memory bank for their images and the feelings they deposited in your heart. If there is any lingering pain, anger, guilt, or shame, you can help release these negative memories by lifting the person up. Place them in a heart-shaped balloon, inflate the balloon with a deep breath of love and forgiveness, and allow them to float away in peace. Trust that you will also feel at peace when you release those people who are weighing heavy on your heart. Take your time, and float as many people as you wish in the love and forgiveness balloons. When you're finished, slowly open your eyes, and bring your peaceful feelings back into the present moment." She paused then asked, "How do you feel, Danny-Boy?"

"I feel like a helium balloon, and I hope I don't pop," he joked, a little nervous about what she was asking him to do.

"Well, that's not necessarily a bad thing because helium will help lighten your emotional load, and if you do pop, that could be considered a breakthrough. If you would like to experience some deeper healing, you can practice this love and forgiveness visualization with anyone at any time. You don't have to wait until your memorial. In fact, we should all be inflating heart-shaped, love-and-forgiveness balloons every day. It helps to keep our mind clear of the emotional stress and our heart clear of the dark patches. If someone is getting on your nerves, Danny-Boy, take a deep breath and float them away. Sometimes, it might feel like a person is plugged into your emotions and stealing your energy. In these cases, you can visualize cutting the cord so you can release them and float them away. You can do this at work, on the bus, at a social gathering…" She laughed then added, "Or even while volunteering at a hospice full of sick kids."

Daniel opened his eyes. "Oh, Angel, you always make everything sound so easy—just float my troubles away. I don't mean to sound like a pessimist, but the harsh reality is the world can be a cruel place to live.

There are too many mean-spirited people out there with bad intentions and evil convictions."

Angel reached and grabbed her iPad off her nightstand. After a couple minutes, she looked up at him and shook her head. "Pinky tells me that a pessimist is the opposite of an optimist."

"Which I guess makes you and I opposites," he told her, "but that's okay. As they say, opposites do attract."

"Danny-Boy, I like to think of our friendship as Red and Sox because Red is young and cute, and Sox is, well, you know…"

"I know. Sox is a little older, a little wiser, and a little more deserving of love. But I guess we all deserve more love, especially in a world that has too much hate."

"You're right; we all deserve more love, and we also need to protect ourselves from the haters and the people who try to harm us. I have been lucky, Daniel, because I haven't experienced hateful feelings. But I read a sad story about a girl who was teased and bullied online until she couldn't take it anymore, and she committed suicide." She looked at him with tears in her big blue eyes. "How could people be so mean?"

"I'm sorry you were exposed to such a tragic story, Angel." He could imagine how reading that story had hurt her soft, kind heart. "But that's what I meant by the harsh reality of life. Those types of sad events—and even worse—happen every day around the world. I don't mean to sound like a pessimist, but we can't expect heart-shaped balloons and Luvffirmations to end the suffering."

Angel gave him a piercing stare. "Is someone having second thoughts about the love mission? You may think your light is small, Daniel, but it can make a huge difference in other people's lives. Collectively, our lights can make a huge difference in our dark world. I found this quote online, and maybe it will help shed some light on your doubts.

"Someone by the name of L.R. Knost said, 'Do not be dismayed by the brokenness in the world. All things break. And all things can be mended. Not with time, as they say, but with intention. So, go. Love intentionally, extravagantly, and unconditionally. The broken world waits in darkness for the light that is you.'"

The words were beautiful, but Daniel still had deep reservations. "I don't know, Angel. I want to believe we could change the world with love, but maybe the world is too dark. Maybe it's too late? Maybe the world isn't fixable? I don't want to discourage you or scare you with shocking news reports. But it seems like there are more and more mass shootings, terrorism plots, violent acts, natural disasters, and other tragic events."

"You don't scare me, Danny-Boy, and I'm definitely not discouraged by the bad news, either. In fact, those kinds of reports make me feel more motivated than ever." She leaned forward and took his hand. "We can do this, Daniel, because love will always prevail over darkness. We need to have hope for a better world, trust in our abilities, and have faith in the power of love. As you know, I believe in God, and I believe this higher power is the source of unconditional love. The way we can tap into this source is by remembering we are love. The Luvffirmations and the heart-shaped-balloon visualizations help stimulate the flow of love in our lives. Each time we pray, meditate, visualize, or project love, the power of love within us grows stronger, and we become closer to the source." She squeezed his hand. "So, what's it going to be, Daniel? Do we want a world full of fireflies or a world overrun with cockroaches?"

He smiled at her way of expressing herself. "Well, that was quite the sermon, Preacher Angel. But I guess that's what a pessimist gets when he expresses doubt to an optimist."

"Yep, and I hope you learned your lesson, but since I gave you an earful, I also want to give you a heart-full before you go home. I have a feeling you are going to love this visualization. Have you ever seen people playing soccer while wearing those over-sized beach balls?"

"I have." Daniel laughed. "It's hilarious, watching the players bounce around on the field." He imagined this was yet another thing Angel had seen online.

"It looks like so much fun, Danny-Boy. If I had a chance to go on a make-a-wish trip, that is what I would wish for. I would love to play soccer while wearing one of those big beach balls."

Daniel shook his head. Angel always found joy in the simple things. "I don't know how much soccer you would be playing, but I can definitely picture you bouncing the other kids around the field."

Well, believe it or not, I was a pretty good soccer player when I was younger. Until I got sick, that is... My dad and I used to play all the time in our back yard. He would play goalie, and I would try to score on him.

Unfortunately, he found out the hard way that, although I was small, I had a hard kick. I hit him square in the privates, and he dropped to his knees, moaning and groaning. I felt so bad, even though he kept trying to tell me he was okay."

Daniel laughed, and tears sprang to his eyes. "Oh, Angel, that's hilarious. That must have been one heck of a painful save.

She frowned. "It's not funny. I could tell I really hurt him." She sighed and shook her head. "Anyway, let's get back to the body part that counts—the heart. This visualization will help you protect your heart from personal attacks, and it will help you project more love. It'll also help you turn your love switch on and crank up the power."

"Geez, Angel, that sounds like the super power of all Luvffirmations. But I'm not feeling very powerful right now. In fact, all the angel flights and balloon blowing has drained my energy away." He started to get to his feet. "I'm afraid it's time to say goodnight, kiddo."

"There's no time like the present for love or another love lesson. Stay present, close your eyes, and visualize your heart swelling to the size of a large, heart-shaped ball that surrounds you. This will be your personal-protection ball that can deflect hateful comments, cruel thoughts, emotional bullying, and tormenting behavior. It helps if you imagine seeing all the negative stuff that's directed toward you bounce off the ball."

Daniel sighed and sat back down, but he perched on the edge of the chair, ready to leave as soon as she'd let him. "I feel like I'm bouncing off the walls, trying to get out of here. The pessimism in me is deflating my heart and inflating my escape wings."

She grinned. "I'm glad to hear you have wings, Danny-Boy, because eventually, those escape wings will be transformed into angel wings. Now, before you fly on out of here, please remember that we are ultimately responsible for protecting and loving ourselves. As you do your Luvffirmations, you can take a deep breath and visualize filling up your heart-shaped protection ball. Try to see yourself walking down the street with your legs, arms, and head sticking out of the ball. People who walk past you won't see it, but they will definitely feel it. Especially animals, because they can sense love from far away. You might get a few cats and dogs sniffing at your heels, while exchanging love with wagging tails and purring sounds. Your heart will be extending out all around you, and not only will your love switch be turned on, but you will be lighting up like a firefly on steroids! How does that sound, Lover-boy?"

"Oh, so now I'm a lover-boy, am I? Well this lover-boy is going to take a deep breath and bounce my inflated heart on out of here!" Again, he got to his feet, intending to make good on his escape this time.

"I'm glad I could bounce this love lesson off you before you go because if you fill up your heart with love, it will be easier to blow up all of those heart-shaped, love-and-forgiveness balloons."

She lay back against her pillows. As much as she enjoyed their visits, and as much as she loved to talk, these sessions often wore her out, and at that moment, she looked completely drained.

"I sure could use a friend who is full of hot air to help me blow up all of those heart-shaped balloons," he teased her.

"I would love to help you," she said softly, "but this love and forgiveness visualization is a solo journey for your own healing. But I'd be happy to share a breathing technique to help you inflate your heart and fill up your body with love. It is called the 'breath of love' and it works wonders when you combine it with your Luffirmations. How do you feel Danny-boy? Would you like to breathe some more love into your life?"

"Do I have a choice? Or are you going to try and resuscitate me with this breath of love, no matter what I say?"

"We all have a choice Daniel and it is called the gift of free will for a reason. You can choose to leave now or you can stay and inhale some loving energy."

"Okay, nurse Angel, you have five minutes to perform CPR and then like it or not, I am going to float away."

"You are a patient, patient Danny-boy and I promise to administer this treatment as quickly as possible. Now close your eyes and slowly breathe in through your nose while visualizing small heart-shaped oxygen bubbles filling your belly and expanding your lungs. Picture the heart-shaped bubbles entering your blood stream and flowing to every cell in your body. As you repeat I am love while breathing in love, you will experience euphoric feelings and miraculous healings."

"Teacher, preacher, or faith healer? I am not sure what to call you tonight."

"Well if you had more faith in your teacher, I wouldn't have to resort to preaching. But, since practice builds faith, let's breath in some love, together. Get comfortable, close your eyes, and slowly inhale those beautiful heart-shaped bubbles"

Daniel kept his eyes closed, as he struggled to keep his mind open to her guidance. His thoughts drifted from heart-shaped bubbles to concerns about Angel's congested breathing. During the last couple of visits, he'd noticed her breathing was getting worse. He slowly opened his left eye to sneak a peek and he was relieved to notice her eyes were closed. She looked so serene sitting up in the middle of the bed, supported by two big puffy pillows. He wondered what thoughts were flowing through her mind. Was she concerned about her raspy breathing? Was she contemplating her own mortality? A rude sound suddenly shattered the peaceful silence.

"Angel was that you? Did you fart?"

Her eyes flickered, a guilty smile emerged, and tinkling giggles confirmed Daniel's suspicions.

"Sorry my new pills give me gas and by the way, girls don't fart, we toot."

"Is that so, I thought maybe some of those heart-shaped bubbles slipped out. Do I need to get the strawberry air-freshener to cover up your toots?"

"No smarty-pants, it is just a little gas and besides, I'm a sweet little Angel."

"A little gas? It sounded like you were trying to light up the world with natural gas!"

Their tooting comments launched them into fits of laughter. Daniel tried to stifle his laughter for fear of alerting the nurses and waking up the sick kids on the floor. But just as they started to settle down, Angel tooted several more times, resulting in uncontrollable laughter and joyful tears.

"We better quiet down Angel, otherwise the nurses are going to sniff out the source of the raucous." He couldn't help teasing her and Angel graciously welcomed his humor. In these moments, they acted like a kindred big brother and an innocent little sister. "I better get going before the fire alarms start ringing. Thank you for another enlightening and flatulating evening."

"Haha, you better run. But before you go, please promise me you will take this love stuff seriously. The Luvffirmations, the love and forgiveness visualizations, the heart-shaped protection ball, and the breath of love will work miracles in your life and in the lives of others."

Daniel nodded. "I'll do my best," he promised her, "but don't be surprised if you end up in one my heart-shaped balloons."

"Ah, is that because you love me, Danny-Boy?" Her voice seemed to grow weaker by the second.

"Well, since love and forgiveness go hand in hand, I will raise you up with love, and I will gladly accept your apology."

"The feeling is mutual, Daniel, and I gladly accept your apology, too. I think it's time for another truce—a real one this time. After all, we're working together to help light up the world with love."

"Don't you mean raise up the world with love?"

She shook her head. "It's kind of both. If we light up with love, we naturally rise up. I'll tell you how that works next week, okay?"

Daniel nodded and turned to leave.

"Oh, hey, I almost forgot," she said.

He turned back. "What's that?"

"Can you please come and visit me on Sunday afternoon at about three o'clock?"

He thought about it a moment and then nodded. "I think I could make that work, Angel, but why Sunday?"

"Well, for the last few years, my dad and I have always watched the Super Bowl together. It's his favorite sport, and he's been teaching me all about the game, ever since I was old enough to sit on his lap and watch sports. It's our special, father/daughter time, only this Sunday, my dad will be away on business. He told my mom he would cancel his trip, but she told him to go so he could be home for the rest of the spring. It was a real dilemma for him, but I told him to go, too, and I told him we could watch the replay of the game on my iPad when he gets back."

"I would love to watch the game with you this Sunday. I might even bring some Super Bowl treats. Do you think your tummy could handle cheese Doritos and strawberry milkshakes?"

Angel brightened a little bit. "Oh, I would love that, Daniel. I am so excited because my favorite quarterback is playing in Super Bowl LII."

"So, you're a Nick Foles fan?"

"Nick Foles? Isn't he a backup quarterback for the Eagles? My dad and I are Patriots fans, and we love Tom Brady. He's won the most Super Bowl rings, and he's cute, too. My dad says that's the only reason I became a Patriots fan, and he might be right." She smiled weakly.

"So, what do you know about football?"

"I know enough about the game to make a wager with you. That is, if you are willing to bet against our team. What do you say, Daniel, Eagles or bust?"

This bet was a no brainer, and Daniel nodded. "Sure, I'll make a bet with you, as long as you're not a sore loser. I heard that Patriots fans struggle with big losses, and there is nothing bigger than a loss at the Super Bowl."

"Oh, Danny-Boy, with comments like that, I'm sure there will be a big love lesson for you and the rest of the Eagles fans next week. Since I'm too young to have a bank account, and since you've been spending your hard-earned money on strawberry milkshakes and other sweet gifts, I think we should make our bet fun. I propose that when my Patriots win, you have to sing *Mary Had a Little Lamb* to the kids in the common room."

You sound pretty confident, but what you don't realize is that your "old man Brady" is going to be up against the best defense in the league. I'll happily take your bet, and I propose that when your Patriots get shut down, you have to sing *All You Need is Love* to the kids and nurses following the game." He gave her a little wave. "And now, I better get going so you can Google the lyrics, and practice singing a few bars."

"I'm not worried, but you should be concerned because those sick kids might laugh you out of the hospice. This is going to be an easy victory for me and my cute QB Brady"

"Oh, geez... Now it's *definitely* time for me to blitz out of here. Night, night, Angel, sleep tight, and don't let the hungry Eagles bite!"

"Love on, Danny-Boy, love on," she murmured.

As Daniel made his escape down the hallway, he was glad the evening ended with some playful bantering. The conversation had been getting pretty deep—or maybe a bit too high—for him. He was learning to trust Angel's advice and insights, even though she was only seven years old. He could relate to the memorial visualization because following the accident, he had contemplated suicide. That time had been one of the lowest points in his life. He recalled feeling trapped in the holding cell with his grieving thoughts for the loss of the little girl. He'd wanted to escape the enduring guilt and shame. He'd wanted to punish himself for taking a young, innocent life. He'd thought about what others would say at his memorial, and he had been concerned that people would call him a coward. The thought of taking his own life had slipped away when his mother showed up at the police station in a fit of concern and care. He remembered her nurturing hug and the reassuring words she'd whispered in his ear. He never did tell her he'd thought about killing himself. He wanted to protect his mother from any more emotional suffering. He tried to bury those morbid thoughts in the past, but tonight's visit with Angel had unearthed the painful memories.

Despite the fact he was facing those painful thoughts again, he decided not to tell Angel how he'd felt back then, either. What good would it do? She was helping him cleanse his soul, and he wanted to protect her from his dirty, depressing secret. That he'd even considered doing such a thing made him feel ashamed and embarrassed, and she might not understand how someone could sink so low in their life. Angel was lifting him up and inspiring him to appreciate everyone and everything. For someone who didn't have much time left, she was so full of love and life. Maybe her terminal prognosis had given her a higher perspective on the power of love and the value of living. He was grateful for her mentoring, and he was thankful for his first "Angel flight." The idea of inflating heart-shaped balloons could only be a reflection of her child-like innocence. Promoting love and forgiveness was a confirmation of her angelic nature.

*****

All the next day, Daniel tried to follow Angel's latest advice. He hadn't realized how many people were weighing heavy on his heart. Every time he closed his eyes and really thought about it, he would see more people in his field of vision. Some of these people were standing right in front of him. His overbearing supervisor at work kept testing Daniel's patience and pushing his stress buttons. If Daniel made a mistake in the morning, his supervisor would hound him for the rest of the day. He would go home at night feeling sick and tired from the stress at work. He felt a sense of relief the first time he visualized his supervisor in a heart-shaped balloon. A weight lifted off his heart when he inflated the balloon with love and forgiveness and floated him away. Would the calmness last until he returned to work the next week? Would this new technique really make a difference? Would his supervisor's overbearing nature bother him like it had in the past? Daniel actually felt sorry for the man and said a little prayer for his supervisor to find more peace in his mind and compassion in his heart. It was a small breakthrough for Daniel, but the big test for the love and forgiveness visualization rested with his father.

Earlier that week, Daniel had surprised his mother by inviting her out to dinner with him that Saturday. As he got ready for their "date," he could barely contain his excitement. She'd sounded so happy when he'd asked her to join him at a little diner near her home, which had made Daniel feel a tiny bit guilty. He'd been living like a hermit since his release from prison, and his reclusive behavior had obviously had a detrimental effect on his mother's mood. But up until recently, he'd been too ashamed and embarrassed to go out in public much. For Daniel to go out to eat at a place that was located in his old neighborhood was a big step. He was breaking his self-imposed chains of solitude and reclaiming his freedom. He'd hesitated to ask his mother to do the driving on their dinner date, but the alternative was taking the bus. So, Daniel had swallowed his pride and asked his mom for a ride.

She had agreed immediately. No big surprise there. She loved cruising around their little town in her blue, 1970 Mustang. She'd even given the old car a name—"Baby Blue"—years ago, when she'd first started driving the car. The Mustang had been the only thing of value she'd received in the divorce. The car had been the old man's pride and joy, but when Good Ol' Dad had walked out on his family, the judge had forced him to give up his classic car. Daniel had been too young at the time to understand the complexities of his parents' breakup. Years later, he'd found out they didn't have many assets to divide up. They'd lost their home to the bank because his dad defaulted on the mortgage. The court awarded the car to his mother along with monthly support payments—payments she never received. His mother deserved better. After his dad abandoned them and left them in financial ruin, they were forced to move several times to find an affordable place to live. She showed him how to survive against adversity, that was certain. She took great pleasure in driving that old car, but why hadn't she ever pursued the delinquent child support payments she was legally owed?

Daniel squinted through the smudged basement window, watching his mom carefully park on the street out front. That car is older than I am, he thought. Talk about ironic! But Mom kept the classic Mustang in mint condition, which no doubt increased its value. She'd already turned down several offers from envious local car collectors. Secretly, he was glad she didn't sell it, but he didn't know why. Did the car represent the only remaining physical connection to his deadbeat dad? Or was it a reminder of how his mother had been treated unfairly after the divorce? A classic car was no substitute for the emotional and financial hardships she'd endured. At least she looked happy behind the wheel of her Baby Blue.

Daniel grabbed a jacket and rushed out to meet his mom. He pulled on the handle, and the passenger door swung open with a welcoming creak. He settled into the soft leather seat and inhaled the familiar scent of a pine air freshener. For a moment, his childhood memories came flooding back—in particular, a happy recollection of going for ice cream with his dad on Saturday morning. Suddenly, another less-joyful memory intruded. Daniel saw himself as a child of no more than four or five, sitting in the back seat of this same car, covering his ears, clinging to Sox, and fearing for his mother, as his father screamed insulting remarks at her.

"Hey." His mother put a hand on his shoulder. "Are you okay?"

Daniel shifted away a little so she wouldn't notice he was shaking and flashed her a smile. "I'm fine, Mom. Just hungry, that's all."

She put the car in gear. "Okay, then let's go eat. I'm pretty hungry, myself, and I can't wait to hear about your week."

As she pulled out and headed toward the intersection, Daniel fought to rid his mind of the troublesome thoughts and relax.

"What's that?" His mom nodded toward the bag in his lap.

"Oh, yeah! I'm glad you reminded me. Will you please swing by the hospice so I can drop this off? It's a little present I bought for Angel. I don't even have to go up; I can just leave it at the front desk." He fingered the paper bag, imagining the look on his friend's face when he opened her gift. The thought made him smile and drove away the bad feelings brought on by the memory of his mom and dad's fight.

*****

Thirty minutes later, Daniel and his mom were settled across from each other at a table at Sally's Diner, a restaurant they'd been patronizing since Daniel was a kid.

"So, tell me how things have been going with your visits with Angel. You saw her yesterday, right?" his mother asked.

The waitress had just brought their plates—Daniel had ordered a hot turkey sandwich with gravy and mashed potatoes, and his mom had ordered a BLT on wheat bread with chips on the side...the same thing she'd always ordered back when they used to visit this diner at least once a week.

"Angel is an amazing person, Mom," he said, scooping up a forkful of potatoes. "She's wise beyond her years...way beyond her years. If I didn't know better, I would think she'd lived a dozen lifetimes. She's got a lot of ideas, and while most of them seem pretty wild on the surface, the way she explains things, they actually make a lot of sense."

His mom nodded. "I knew that little girl was special from the minute you first told me about her. I saw such a big difference in your attitude and mood, and I could only thank God for bringing her into your life."

"She's taught me a lot of interesting things, that's for sure," he said around a mouthful of turkey and gravy. He chewed and swallowed before telling her about the love and forgiveness visualization techniques. "Basically, I just picture the person inside a heart-shaped frame or a heart-shaped balloon, and depending upon the situation, I either ask for forgiveness or send messages of love and forgiveness and release the balloon into the air." He smiled sheepishly, imagining how crazy he sounded. But doggone it, these "crazy" techniques really seemed to have made a difference in his life.

His mom nibbled on a potato chip, a thoughtful look on her face. "So, you can ask someone to forgive you, or you can forgive someone else just by picturing them inside a heart-shaped frame or balloon and...what? Sending them telepathic messages?"

Daniel nodded. "Yes, that's pretty much how it works—and it really does work." The moment he finished speaking, Daniel wished he could take back the words. Now, he'd be forced to explain *why* he thought the technique worked. He tried to think of something else to say to keep his mom from asking the next obvious question, but she didn't give him a chance to change the subject.

"How could you possibly—? Oh! The phone call from your father!"

Daniel glanced around the room, afraid his mother's loudly voiced statement had attracted unwanted attention, but no one seemed to be paying any mind to their conversation. "Shh… Mom, please… I'd rather not share our personal business with everyone in town."

His mother dabbed her mouth with her napkin then placed it back onto her lap. "I'm sorry, Daniel. I didn't mean to shout; I was just surprised and excited, that's all." She sighed and picked up another potato chip. "You can't imagine how much I've worried about the situation between you and your dad. I realize he hurt you—"

"Not just me, Mom. He left *both* of us," Daniel said softly. "He *hurt* both of us."

His mom reached across the table and put her hand on his. "True, but Daniel, I was an adult, and you were just a little boy. We both struggled after your father left, but I'm sure you had a more difficult time handling his disappearance from our lives than I did. You were young and confused, and while I came to terms with what happened between your dad and me, I don't think you've ever gotten over losing your daddy."

Daniel couldn't speak. His eyes burned, and his throat felt thick, as if it were swollen shut. He grabbed his ice water and took a long swallow.

"So, I take it I was right? You tried this forgiveness technique with your dad, and then all of the sudden, he's calling and wanting to see you?" she asked him, squeezing his hand. "It's okay, you know? You're not going to hurt my feelings if you want to try to heal or reestablish a relationship with your father."

Daniel shook his head. "No way," he said adamantly. "And I promise it has nothing to do with you. I just… There's just no place in my life for him right now. But Angel helped me realize that the pain and anger I've been carrying around all these years has been hurting me and keeping me from being the kind of person I want to be. By not forgiving Dad, I've only been hurting myself."

His mom stared at him for a few moments and then nodded, as if she'd reached some decision. She gestured toward his half-eaten turkey. "Eat up," she said, picking up half of her BLT. "This food's too good to let go to waste."

Daniel nodded and resumed eating his meal, thankful she'd decided to drop the subject. Even though he was doing his best to release the hurtful feelings involving his father, Daniel still had a hard time discussing the past, and he really wanted to end this meal on a high note.

They finished eating, ordered pie and coffee for dessert, and spent the next half hour making small talk. By the time his mom pulled up in front of his basement apartment to drop him off, he'd managed to regain his balance and good humor. He kissed his mom's cheek and gave her a hug.

"Thanks for dinner," she told him.

Daniel pulled his house key from his pocket. "Thank you for coming with me. We'll do it again soon."

He climbed out of her car and waved good-bye, surprised to realize he actually *was* looking forward to going out again. Two months ago, nothing could have gotten him to show his face in a local restaurant. A lot had changed for him in the last eight weeks, and he had one person to thank for bringing him back to the world of the living. As he let himself inside his apartment, he sent up a silent prayer of thanks to whatever higher power had brought Angel into his life.

SUPER BOWL SUNDAY

Daniel felt out of place walking into the hospice on a Sunday afternoon. He was used to the Friday-night visits, but this week was a special occasion, and he was looking forward to watching the Super Bowl with his little Angel. He decided to hide the gym bag with the banned treats and another special surprise in Angel's empty room. She would be waiting to watch the big game in the family room with a bunch of rowdy kids and chaperoning nurses. As he headed toward the visiting area, he wondered how Angel had liked the present he'd left for her the previous night.

Sounds of excitement streamed down the hallway, signaling that the kids were cranked up before the official kickoff. He proudly strutted into the room, wearing his Eagles jersey, only to be welcomed by an awkward silence, blank stares, and a room full of hand-drawn Patriots pictures and slogans. He knew immediately that Angel had quarter-backed the decorating, and she was directing the plays for the kids. He felt like a lone, vulnerable Eagles fan trapped in a room full of rowdy Patriot fans. If he was connected to social media, he would have had fun tweeting some of the kid's uniquely inspirational slogans, such as, *Patriots clip the wings of the Eagles*, and *Dear Nick Foles, thanks for the sixth Super Bowl ring, signed Tom Brady, MVP*. These sarcastic sayings had Angel's humor written all over them.

Daniel glanced around the room until he caught her attention. She was huddled in the middle of a group of other children, surrounded by an innocent-looking group of cheering Patriots fans.

Daniel groaned inwardly. This was sure to be a long and loud afternoon. Only then did he spot the special gift he'd dropped off the night before, and he had to laugh. Apparently, Angel had gotten her hands on some snacks, and she'd filled the brand-new, Eagles cap with what looked like pretzels and hot-buttered popcorn. She held out the cap, and the hungry kids sitting beside her dug in, scooping out handfuls of popcorn and pretzels and chewing happily. Daniel shook his head in defeat. She had desecrated his team's hat, but she looked so happy, so pleased with herself, he couldn't bring himself to care. Nor was he surprised by her tactics. In fact, he'd pretty much expected to find the Eagles hat in some sort of compromised condition. But boy, he wished he could have been there to see Angel's expression when she first opened the gift. He silently applauded her resourcefulness at using the hat as a popcorn bowl, but he wasn't going to give her the satisfaction of watching him eat out of it. That would have been a sign of weakness; instead, Daniel would wait and take satisfaction when the Eagles swooped down and won the game today.

*****

In the end, Daniel's team didn't let him down. Although it was a close and entertaining game, the underdog Eagles clawed a victory away from the favored New England Patriots. Daniel sat there with a purposely smug smile on his face, knowing his expression was driving Angel crazy. She tried in vain to rally her kid cheerleaders, but their lack of interest in a three-hour-long football game resulted in a bunch of bored children roaming around in the family room, talking and laughing with one another and mostly ignoring the game.

The loudest cheers occurred during the halftime show, and this excitement set the stage for Angel's encore entertainment. As the Eagles were celebrating their Super Bowl win, Angel stood up and sang her losing-bet song.

Daniel listened quietly, impressed to learn she knew all the lyrics to the famous Beatle's song, *All You Need is Love*. The kids and the nurses cheered her on, and in a show of good sportsmanship, Daniel joined her in singing the chorus. It was the perfect end to a fun Super Bowl party.

Afterward, the patient nurses ushered the tired kids back to their rooms. Daniel volunteered to escort Angel back to hers, and during their silent walk down the hallway, he sealed his team's victory with one last kick at his opponent.

"Well, kid, that was fun. I'm glad you got to witness my young backup QB become the Super Bowl MVP. Maybe it's time for your old QB to retire."

Angel looked up at him and batted her eyelashes. "Daniel, do you want your Eagle's hat back, or should I keep it as an emergency barf bag?" she asked sweetly.

Daniel shrugged. "You can do whatever you like with that hat. It was my special gift for you, and besides, I won't need it. I'll be adding a new, Eagles Super Bowl LII hat to *my* collection."

"Okay," she huffed, "that'll be enough smug victory comments out of you tonight. I'm getting tired, and I think it's time to float you away in a love-and-forgiveness balloon."

Daniel laughed. "Is that your polite way of saying good night? I thought for sure you'd have another love lesson for me this week."

As they reached her room, Angel stopped, put her hands on her hips, and stared up at him for a moment. Finally, she nodded. "Fine. To prove I'm a good sport and to protect our friendship, I'll share a timely love lesson with you and all the other Eagles fans. While it's important to celebrate our successes and victories in life, it's imperative to remain humble and kind. Humbleness and kindness are signs that our love switch is turned on."

"Uh huh," Daniel said skeptically. "I can't help but wonder if you'd be sharing this particular love lesson with me right now if your Patriots had been lucky enough to win?"

"Yes, I would have," she said and then laughed. "But I'd probably wait a week so I could rub your nose in the fact that my team had won."

"Ah, so the moral of this love lesson is 'do what I say and not as I do'?"

Angel shrugged, and Daniel shook his head.

"Come on, let's get you into bed. We have a couple of strawberry milkshakes waiting for us, and by now, they're probably more like strawberry milk."

He took her hand and helped her up into her bed, then made sure she was propped up with a stack of pillows. He then shrugged the backpack off his shoulders and set it on the blue-vinyl chair.

"I've been thinking about those strawberry shakes, and I have an idea."

"What's that?" he asked, unzipping the bag and reaching in to pull out the no-doubt-melted shakes.

"Well, before we get to that, there's something else I want to talk to you about."

He held out one of the shakes to her, but she shook her head.

"No. Not yet. If you don't mind, let's wait until after we've had our talk before we drink those."

Daniel shrugged. "They can't melt any more than they already have, I guess." He set the cups on her nightstand, placed his backpack on the floor, and took a seat. "Okay, what do you want to talk about?" he asked, then held up a hand. "Just please…let's not talk about my dad tonight, okay? I've had enough of that topic for a while."

Angel shook her head. "No…we won't talk about your daddy issues. There's something else we need to discuss." She glanced away. "I've been avoiding having this conversation with you, but the time is right, and I think you are ready to listen and learn."

"Now you have my curiosity on high alert. I'm listening, Angel; what do you want to talk about?"

She looked back at him and held his gaze. "Death," she said. "I want to talk about death. You know I'm dying, right? We've touched on the subject during a few of our visits, but we've never had a heart-to-heart chat. Are you okay with talking about death and mortality?"

Daniel took a deep breath in a desperate attempt to suppress his emotions. He remembered how candid and brave she was during their first visit, when she'd told him—a complete stranger at the time—about her terminal cancer. During the last eight weeks, he'd sadly noticed her declining health. She was slipping away from this world, but he wasn't emotionally prepared to let her go. Her humor lifted his spirits. Her antics at the Super Bowl party brought joy to his heart. Her question hit him like a fist in the stomach, and he doubled over in pain, no longer able to hold back his tears.

To Daniel's horror, he began sobbing like a little kid who'd just lost his favorite toy. He gasped for breath, struggling to regain control. Morbid images of a child's still body flashed across his mind. The reality of losing his sweet little Angel pierced his heart.

Angel leaned to put a hand on his trembling shoulder. "I'm sorry," she said. "I didn't mean to make you sad. But it's okay, Daniel…you don't have to be embarrassed to cry in front of me. My parents try to cover up their tears, especially my dad, but I can always tell when he's about to break down because he makes up an excuse to step out of my room. At first, I thought he had a bladder problem. He would disappear into my bathroom, or he would flee down the hall to the visitors' washroom. He usually returns to my room with red eyes and his hat pulled down to cover his sadness." She patted Daniel's shoulder and sighed. "I wish he *could* cry in front of me. I wish he could share his emotions with me. Sometimes, my mom cuts our visit short so she can usher away my basket-case dad. I asked one of the nurses, and she told me most men don't like to show their sad emotions. Why are you guys embarrassed to cry, Daniel?"

He drew in a deep, shaky breath and wiped at his eyes. "I don't know how to answer that. I can't speak for every man, but I don't like crying in front of other people because I've always heard it's a sign of weakness. Plus, I don't like crying in front of you because I don't want to make you feel any worse than you already do."

"Seeing you cry doesn't make me feel worse; it tells me you care. We can't bottle up our emotions, Danny-Boy. There is nothing embarrassing about showing the depth of our emotions with tears. They're meant to flow, and when they do, they help us grow." She paused and smiled at him. "Maybe that's why women are more advanced than men? And maybe that's why women live longer than men? Except, of course, for some of us terminally ill kids. We might only be here for a short time, but we learn to appreciate our time on Earth. Are you enjoying your time here, Daniel?"

"Do you mean here, as in visiting with you? Because I love spending time with you."

"Well, I'm happy to hear that, but are you also enjoying your time here on Earth?"

Daniel gave a shaky laugh. "You make it sound like we're just passing through."

Angel nodded. "In a way, we're on a life journey, and Earth is an important stop for the development and growth of our soul. I have to learn fast because my days on Earth are limited, but you've been blessed with more time in the classroom, and I hope you're grateful for it."

"I'm not sure about the classroom time, but I am grateful for one of my young teachers."

"Well, this young teacher is grateful to have such an open-minded and open-hearted student, especially one who brings his teacher treats every week!" She sat back on her pillows and drew in a deep breath. "Okay...I want to talk to you about my feelings on death. If you feel like you need to cry, please don't be embarrassed. I believe a man who cries is a man worth caring for, and if you don't know by now, I really care about you."

"I feel the same way about you." Daniel had managed to regain his composure, and he injected a note of strength into his voice. "Go ahead and talk. After all this time, I don't think there's much you could say that would make me feel uncomfortable." He nodded toward her nightstand. "Why don't we drink those now?"

Angel shook her head. "Thank you, but not tonight. You can drink yours, but as I mentioned earlier, I have an idea to share with you." She glanced toward her window. "There's a homeless man living behind the hospice. I've seen him out there just about every day, and I feel so sad for him. Sometimes, he wanders onto the grounds, searching for cans and food in the garbage bins. The security staff have chased him away on several occasions. He rushes off into the woods, and I think he has camp set up there. I've seen smoke rise from the bushes, and I've watched him drag a shopping cart full of stuff along an overgrown path through the trees. It must be so cold and wet at night, and I wish I could help him out."

Daniel's eyes stung with unshed tears. "You really are a sweet angel. You have a kind soul, and I'm sure you would do anything you could do to help this homeless man. I feel sad when I see people struggling to survive on the streets. Our world must seem like a cruel place for those who are down on their luck."

"It's not only bad luck; it's a tragedy to see so many human souls lost in poverty and despair in a world of unbalanced prosperity. Can't we learn to share our wealth and resources more fairly, Daniel? The reality TV programs that show off the extravagant, wealthy lifestyles of the rich and famous make me feel sick to my stomach. When I stream the news, I see the reality of poverty and sickness in our world. Some days, I just want to turn off Pinky and dream of a better world. I don't understand why things are so messed up? If kids ruled the world, we'd share and care. If I had more time here, I would dedicate my life to making the world a better place for everyone, including Mother Earth and all of her beautiful creatures!"

"You have a big, compassionate heart, Angel, and I wish you had more time to fulfill your dreams."

"Oh, but I *do* have enough time, Daniel, because you agreed to help me lovify the world. You do remember our pact, don't you?" she asked sweetly.

Pact? When had they made a pact? Daniel frowned. "Sorry, but I don't recall making a pact with you."

"Hmm, you know what? You're right. We never did formalize our love mission, did we?" Angel reached over and grabbed her iPad off her nightstand. "Well, if we're going to light up the world with love—or lovify the world—then we need to make it official. We also need to make it fun and give it a cool name. How about, *The Quest to Lovify the World*? How does that sound, Danny-Boy?"

"It sounds like you have a great imagination, and you'd make a great director or producer, but I'm not sure I'm the right actor to carry out a love quest." He still couldn't bring himself to tell her what he knew she wanted to hear, mostly because he feared he'd let her down.

"Don't worry, Daniel, I'll make sure you are well-versed and properly prepared before I go…and after I am gone."

Daniel shivered dramatically. "Geez, that last bit sounded a bit creepy, Angel. Are you planning on coming back and haunting me, or will you only direct me from above?" He honestly couldn't believe they were having this conversation. How could she reference her own death in such a nonchalant way? If he was dying, he sure as heck wouldn't be joking about it. Then again, knowing Angel, she wasn't kidding around about this. She definitely sounded serious.

"I'll only come back and haunt you if you abandon the quest. If you follow my lead, Daniel, you won't have anything to worry about. In fact, I think we should seal our pact tonight by making a Pinky swear."

"A pinky swear?" Daniel laughed. "Are you serious? How old are you, kid?"

"I'm old enough to know that a Pinky swear, made in good faith, is the best way to seal our pact and to keep you on track. Plus, I've come up with my own version of the Pinky swear that I think you'll appreciate."

Daniel could just imagine. When it came to creativity, Angel had other kids beat, hands down. "Okay, what's this unique version you've come up with?" He leaned forward, ready to join pinky-fingers with Angel and make a pact.

Angel placed her iPad on her lap. "Well, since we're doing a Pinky swear, we can join our pinky fingers on top of Pinky. She'll be the witness to our pact. Too bad we don't have Red and Sox here to witness our pact, too."

Daniel sat back. "Oh, shoot! That reminds me. Talk about synchronistic timing. Guess what special surprise I brought for you tonight." He leaned down and opened up his backpack again.

"Real strawberries to put on top of our milkshakes?" she asked hopefully. "If that's the case, I may change my mind about the idea I have."

"No, sorry. I didn't think of that, and what do strawberries have to do with your idea…? You still haven't told me what that is, you know?" He straightened, hiding his surprise beneath his hands on his lap.

"All in good time, Danny-Boy. All in good time." She craned her neck. "What have you got there?"

Daniel held up the sock puppet his grandmother had made him. "I brought Sox with me tonight so she could meet you and Red."

For a moment, Angel stared at Sox, her eyes wide, and then she began to giggle. She continued to stare as her giggles turned into full-blown laughter.

What the heck? Daniel had thought Angel would be delighted to finally meet his beloved, childhood friend, but he hadn't counted on her laughing her butt off. "Hey! What's the deal!" he asked her, looking back and forth between her and Sox.

"Danny-Boy, that is the saddest-looking sock puppet I've ever seen!" Angel wiped tears from her eyes and continued to giggle. "Your Sox is full of holes! What have you been doing, wearing her on your feet?"

Daniel huffed. How dare she make fun of his Sox? "No, I have not been wearing her on my feet, and I'm sorry you think my Sox looks funny. She *is* old, you know. Older than you, even!"

Angel hiccupped a few times, putting a hand to her mouth and stifling her laughter. "Okay, Daniel; you're right. I shouldn't make fun of your Sox. Especially since you were kind enough—and brave enough—to bring her out into public." She let loose another series of giggles.

"I'm beginning to regret my decision to bring her here." Daniel scowled. "Let's get this pinky-swear thing over with so I can take Sox home and fix a few of her holes. Then maybe next week, she'll be more presentable, and we can introduce her to Red."

"I'm not sure a needle and thread is going to do the trick," she told him. "You might need a whole new pair of socks to fix your old Sox. But I agree, we should complete our Pinky swear." She nodded toward her nightstand. "Please put Sox over there beside Red—they can also be witnesses—and then let's hook pinky-fingers."

Daniel did as she requested, feeling a bit silly, but yet, at the same time, sensing the underlying gravity of the situation. Typical of his dealings with Angel these past several weeks... Once he'd hooked his pinky finger with Angel's, she looked at him and nodded.

"Okay, now, repeat after me," she said. "I, Daniel, do solemnly swear to uphold this pact with Angel, to carry out The Quest to Lovify the World, until death joins us together."

Daniel repeated her words, but then added, "You've obviously given a lot of thought to this, but I didn't hear you swear to your part?"

"Hmm. True." She nodded. "Okay, give me your pinky finger again."

Once they'd joined fingers again, she smiled.

"Here's my promise to you. I, your *sweet, loving* Angel, do solemnly swear to uphold a pact with Daniel"—she glanced over at her nightstand and giggled—"and his old, holey Sox, to guide him on the love quest." She paused, then added, "And to haunt him if he breaks our pact, until death joins us together." She eyed him and grinned. "How does that sound, Daniel?"

"I'm not surprised to hear that your part of the pact is a little more colorful than mine. But I guess I shouldn't expect anything less from a hairless kid with a colorful wig." He shook his head and leaned back in his chair.

"Touché, Daniel! Great comeback." She frowned at him. "But I think your love switch turned off—remember, I lost my hair because I have cancer..." She smiled at him. "Fortunately for you, I have a way to help you turn your love switch back on."

"I think it's time for me to go." Emotionally drained, Daniel got to his feet. "You can share your idea with me next time." He paused then added, "Oh, by the way, I won't be able to visit you on Friday night."

Angel frowned. "Was it something I said? You aren't angry with me, are you?"

"No, sweet Angel, I'm not mad at you. My mother wants to take me out for dinner to celebrate the official end of my probation period. But I'll come and visit you the following week if that is okay. Promise!"

Angel sighed dramatically. "I'll have to check my busy social schedule, but I'm sure I can fit you in." She sat up, her expression turning serious. "Please, don't go yet, Daniel, I need to share my idea with you *tonight* because as you know—"

"Yes, I know…" He interrupted her. "Life is too short not to love. Okay, share away, but please, make it quick." He nodded toward her nightstand. "I think Sox is getting cold."

Angel laughed. "I can't imagine why, Daniel. The poor thing is full of holes!"

He scowled at her, and she immediately sobered.

"I'm sorry," she said. "I guess I better be nice because I have a big favor to ask you. Like I said earlier, I feel really bad for that homeless man, so I've been saving my rice puddings all week. You know how I love those rice puddings." Her words were laced with sarcasm, and she grimaced. "Anyways, it would mean the world to me if you could deliver them, along with my strawberry milkshake, to the man in the woods. You can tell him an angel sent you."

Oh, boy… The mere thought of fulfilling her request made Daniel's hands shake. "Um, no…" He shook his head. "I'm sorry, kid, but I'm not comfortable doing that. Don't get me wrong; it's a really sweet, generous idea, but how do you know he's even in the woods tonight, and what if he's violent or crazy or something?"

Angel nodded toward her window. "If you look out there, you'll see the smoke from his camp. It doesn't look like it's too far from the fence line, and I'm pretty sure he's harmless. I waved to him one time when he was crossing through the yard. He waved back at me and smiled. I think he's lonely, Daniel, and I'm sure he's hungry. Please do this for me, Daniel; it will make me feel better, it will help the homeless man feel better, and I guarantee you'll feel better, too, for carrying out such a generous act of kindness."

Daniel glanced toward the window then back at Angel. She would never give up on the idea. Once she got something into her head, she held on to it like a dog with a bone. He heaved a sigh, wondering what he was getting himself into. "Okay, okay, I'll do it. But are you sure you want to give away your strawberry milkshake? I brought that treat for you because I know how much you love them."

"And as always, I'm grateful for your generosity." She gave him a beaming smile. "But it would make me feel better to extend that generosity to someone who would really enjoy it. I feel bad that all I have to offer him are those crappy rice puddings, so I figure I can make up for it a little, by giving him the milkshake to wash them down with."

"By the time he gets that milkshake, it'll be strawberry mush, I'm sure, but I guess it'll still taste good." Daniel thought for a moment about what he was agreeing to do and then nodded. "All right, I'll deliver the food, but if you don't see me again, you might want to send out a search party to look for my body in the woods," he added, only half-joking.

"Geez, way to make me feel guilty about sending you on a generosity mission." Angel huffed and crossed her arms. "You know, Daniel, if we're going to carry out the love quest, then you're going to have to learn to trust me. You do trust me, don't you, Danny-Boy?"

"You've asked me that question a dozen times before, and I assume this generosity mission is some kind of test to prove my trust in you." He sighed dramatically. "I'll do my best to carry out your request. Now…where are those puddings? If I'm going to catch the next bus, I'll need to get moving."

"They're in a bag under my bed. Will you grab them for me?"

Daniel leaned over to reach beneath her bed and pulled out a plastic grocery bag half-filled with rice puddings. He stuffed them, along with Sox and both strawberry milkshakes, into his backpack, careful to situate the shakes so they wouldn't spill.

"You're not going to drink your shake?" she asked, giving him a knowing look.

"You're already aware that I couldn't possibly drink my milkshake when you're giving yours away to a homeless man," he told her. "I guess tonight is his lucky night."

Angel laughed softly. "You're a good man, Daniel." She sighed and closed her eyes. "Now, you better get going before the rice puddings expire…or I do."

Daniel eyed her with concern. She really didn't look well. "Then you better get some rest because I don't want you to expire on me." He carefully laced his arms through the straps on his backpack. "Night, night, kiddo. Sleep tight, and don't let the quarterbacks bite!"

She opened her eyes, and he winked at her.

"The only quarterback who can bite me is my cute QB Brady. Goodnight, Danny-Boy, and remember—remain humble, generous, and kind, and keep your love on!"

Daniel chuckled at Angel's comments. Although she looked like she'd just played a tiring football game, she still managed to show him humor and love.

He blew her a kiss and without another word left her room and headed down the hallway toward the back staircase. The door at the bottom led to the parking lot near the dumpsters and the woods where the homeless man supposedly stayed. Was this mission she'd sent him on really just a test of his trust in her, or was this something more? As Daniel pushed out the door at the bottom of the staircase, he took a deep breath of icy air. He had a gut feeling Angel had just sent him on his first mission as part of their *Quest to Lovify the World*.

As Daniel found the entrance to the half-overgrown path leading into the dark woods, he began to perspire, and his hands were shaking a little. He drew in a deep breath and plunged forward, following the odor of wood smoke as he made his way along the trail. At one point, he paused and considered turning around and abandoning this fool's mission, but then he gathered his courage and moved forward. He didn't want to disappoint Angel, and she would be disappointed in him if he failed her in this task.

Finally, after traveling several hundred yards into the creepy woods, he spotted the homeless man sitting on what looked like a damp tarp and leaning over a sputtering fire.

"Hello?" Daniel called out to the man, not wanting to startle or frighten him by just tramping into the camp. "Excuse me, sir?"

The man looked up from under his dirty hoody. They locked eyes, and Daniel sensed the man's fearful confusion.

"It's okay," he said, taking a few steps closer. "I'm not here to…to hurt you or anything."

The man didn't respond, but he didn't move, either, so Daniel closed the distance between them. He carefully removed his backpack and set it on the ground.

"There's a little girl," he explained. "Um, Angel…and she's a patient at the hospice." He pointed back over his shoulder. "She says she's seen you from her window, and she asked me to bring you something."

"Ah, yes," the man said, his voice gruff. He nodded and smiled. "I know who you mean." He glanced down at the backpack and licked his lips. "What have you got there?"

Daniel leaned over, unzipped the backpack, and pulled out the bag with the rice puddings inside. "Well, there's this," he said, handing the bag to the man. Daniel then carefully extracted both milkshake containers from the backpack and held them out. "And these."

The man's eyes grew wide as he accepted the milkshakes, holding each one up to examine them, as if he'd never seen a fast-food shake container before. Or maybe he just hadn't held one in a long, long time, Daniel thought.

He gazed around the little, makeshift camp, as he contemplated his own good fortune in life. How horrid would it be to call this place home? How did this man survive in such appalling conditions, forced to stay outside in all kinds of weather? Why was the poor guy on his own, and where were his family and friends? Why wasn't he at a local shelter? How could he keep warm on a cool, wet night?

"Nathanial," the man said, interrupting Daniel's thoughts.

For a moment, he didn't understand what the guy was saying, but then it hit him. "Um, my name's Daniel," he said. "Nice to meet you, Nathanial."

The man nodded absently as he opened the bag holding the puddings and pulled out one of the tiny containers, along with a spoon Angel must have stuck in there for him. As Daniel stood silently by, the man ignored him and dug into the pudding, scarfing it down in less than two minutes. God, Daniel thought, what must it be like to be that hungry? For all he knew, Nathanial hadn't eaten in days. He sure acted as if he was starving.

As Daniel struggled for understanding, he also dealt with a mixture of anger and compassion. How had someone's son or brother or father or ex-husband come to find himself living in the woods like this? Daniel shook his head. No…this wasn't living—this was a human being struggling to survive against almost insurmountable odds.

After Nathanial finished off one of the puddings, he stuffed the rest of them—as well as the spoon—inside a grimy, old duffle bag. Daniel didn't want to be nosy, but he was curious, so he peered over the man's shoulder to see what else Nathanial had stashed away. Inside was a plastic bag of moldy-looking buns, some rotten-looking fruit, and what appeared to be a half-empty bottle of liquor. Daniel wasn't surprised at all by the presence of the last item; after all, who knew how he'd behave if he were stuck like this, trying to live under these conditions?

As Daniel considered all of this, Angel's reason for sending him on this mission suddenly became clear to him. *The Quest to Lovify the World* suddenly became *real* for him. Angel had wanted him to understand; this was no little kids' game or a fictional tale. This was real life, and Daniel's heart opened up with love and compassion for a homeless man surviving in the woods.

Nathanial looked up at Daniel and smiled, then took a long drink of one of the strawberry milkshakes. Eyes glowing, the man smacked his lips and nodded before taking another drink. Tears streamed down Daniel's cheeks as he realized how grateful Nathanial was for such a small, simple pleasure. Daniel wished he had something warm to offer, like a hot coffee or hot chocolate or a waterproof tent and a dry blanket. But this was all he had to offer tonight, and Nathanial's sincere appreciation warmed Daniel's heart.

"Well, I guess I'll say good-bye…for now," Daniel said.

Nathanial nodded, but as Daniel picked up his backpack, he had an idea. He reached inside the backpack again and pulled out his sock puppet. Sox might be old and worn out, but maybe she could offer Nathanial a small bit of comfort here in these dark and lonely woods. Daniel turned back and gently placed Sox in Nathanial's callused, dirty hand. He looked up at Daniel, surprise showing in his expression, but then he clutched Sox to his heart, nodded, and resumed sipping on the strawberry milkshake.

Humbled and touched beyond words, Daniel slipped back onto the trail and made his way out of the woods. He rounded the fence line and glanced up at the window just in time to see Angel wave and blow him a kiss. She must have been watching for his exit to make sure he made it out of the woods safely—and with a huge love lesson in tow. The brief encounter with the homeless man would change Daniel for life. He'd been living a selfish existence, caught up in his own guilt and shame. He couldn't change the past, but he could chart a new path. Opening his eyes, mind, and heart was the important first step on his quest to lead a purposeful life. He was not only ready to follow Angel's guidance on The Quest to Lovify the World, he was ready to lead. If it wasn't so late, and if he thought he could get in and out without getting caught, he would have snuck back into the hospice to give Angel a big hug and thank her. He smiled, thinking about their "Pinky swear" and the way Angel had teased him about his old, holey Sox. Wouldn't Angel be shocked when she learned Sox had found a new home, where his cherished sock puppet could give love and comfort to a lonely, old homeless man?

WEEK 8

Daniel woke up Monday morning, his heart pounding with anticipation and excitement. This was his final week of probation and the end of most of his probationary conditions. Although the driving ban was still in effect for another two years, the shackles that had kept him from his freedom and independence were being removed. He could also access the Internet and social media, which would allow him to return to work in the technology field. He was looking forward to submitting his resignation at the call center at the end of the week.

*****

Daniel's first step toward freedom occurred on Wednesday morning. At his final probation meeting, he received the key that would unlock his potential in life. His probation officer advised Daniel to let go of his guilty past, to move forward with confidence, and to make something out of his life by serving others. It was simple advice he knew his mother would approve of and that his little Angel would echo. He could almost hear her ringing endorsement and her loving encouragement.

*****

On Friday morning, Daniel submitted his resignation to his boss. But instead of acting as if he couldn't wait to get out of there—as he'd imagined himself doing a million times when he'd first started working there—he went out of his way to show his supervisor and his coworkers how thankful he was for their patience, support, and understanding. They wished him well in his future endeavors, and they even celebrated his departure with donuts someone had run out and purchased during their afternoon lunch break.

"Thank you. Sincerely," Daniel said, addressing the small crowd of coworkers who'd gathered to say good-bye and wish him well. He smiled sheepishly. "And I'm really sorry I was such a moody beast those first few weeks."

"We've enjoyed having you here," his boss said, patting Daniel on the shoulder. "And *I* apologize, too, if I came off as overly harsh now and then. I've been under a lot of pressure lately, and I guess shit tends to run downhill."

All behavior makes sense, Daniel thought, as he nodded and accepted the man's apology. Had the "love and forgiveness" visualization helped to mend their working relationship?

Later that same day, Daniel walked out of the call center with a sense of relief but also more than a little nervousness. What did his future have in store for him? He was leaving a boring but stable job, and he was opening an uncertain chapter in his life. He had to trust in himself and have faith in his instincts at this point in his journey, especially if he was going to help light up the world with love. He wasn't sure if he was quite ready to accept Angel's invitation for a love quest, but he was willing to keep an open mind and a lighter heart. His first priority was to spend some quality time with the one person who could always light up his heart with maternal love.

*****

Daniel met his mother at the same diner they'd eaten at on their previous dinner date. This time, he'd taken the bus, since his mom had arrived straight from work, which was on the opposite side of town from his place. He smiled when he saw Baby Blue spanning two parking stalls in front of the diner. His mom usually parked on an angle to protect her precious car from careless drivers and their swinging car doors. Would she be comfortable allowing him to drive her car again when he got his license back? He recalled how paranoid she'd been when he'd first started driving. She would sit in the passenger seat and point out the driving hazards, risky drivers, and remind him of all the rules of the road, as he'd cautiously inched along. Sincerely, she was probably just as concerned about his well-being as she was about protecting her Baby Blue. He recalled her relief, even though she tried not to show it, when he got his first car at age nineteen.

Daniel had to pause for a moment before entering the diner. The thought of his old car brought back the horrific images of the accident scene. Guilty feelings invaded his mind. He suddenly felt anxious and nervous. His heart was pounding, sweat beaded on his forehead, and he gasped for breath. A dark, somber mood clouded his judgement, and he contemplated abandoning his dinner date. This was supposed to be a happy celebration with his mom. He thought of Angel, and he took several deep breaths and silently affirmed, *I am love and I forgive and love myself*. Several minutes passed, but finally, a sense of calm filled him, lightening his mood. He took another deep breath, while silently expressing gratitude for the transformation that just occurred. Fully composed, he opened the door and stepped inside, ready to join his mother for dinner.

"I'm so proud of you and so happy for you," she told him, once they'd placed their orders with their waitress. "You're not the same boy you were a couple years ago, and your future is wide open."

"Thanks, Mom," he told her, his cheeks growing warm at her praise. "I'm excited, but I'm also a little freaked out."

"Well, I have something I think will help you regain your balance a little." She reached into her purse and pulled out a small, rectangular box and placed it on the table between them.

"What's that?" he asked, making no move to touch the gift. He had a feeling he knew, but he didn't want to get his hopes up. Still, his heart started racing.

"Just a little present I picked up for you on my lunch hour today." She smiled and nodded toward the box. "Go ahead. Open it."

Hands trembling, Daniel picked up the box and tore off the wrapping paper. As he read the description on the lid, tears streamed down his face, and his chest tightened, his heart overflowing with love for his mother.

"It's awesome," he told her, removing the lid and taking out the brand-new, high-tech smartphone. "If I had to pick one myself, I couldn't have done better." He looked up at her and smiled. "Thanks, Mom."

She nodded, her eyes glistening with unshed tears. "I'm glad you like it. Now put it away. You'll have plenty of time to mess with it—*after* dinner."

Daniel stuffed the phone into his jacket pocket. She was right—he had waited this long; he could wait another hour to get back online, and besides…she deserved his full attention and appreciation. The affection he felt for her was overwhelming.

"I love you, Mom," he said, compelled to share his thoughts. "I mean, I really, really love you. Thank you for always being there for me…for always *believing* in me. You are my best friend in this world."

His mom glanced down, looking a bit uncomfortable. "There's one thing you need to know," she said. "I took the liberty of programming one number into your new cellphone." She looked up at him. "Of course, it'll be up to you if you ever use it."

Daniel knew without asking whose number his mother had given him, and to his surprise, he wasn't upset about it. "It's okay, Mom. Don't worry about it…"

"He wants to come visit you," she told him. "He said he wants to make up for lost time."

Daniel smiled as he silently floated his father away in a love and forgiveness balloon.

"You're not angry with me, are you?" she asked him.

He shook his head. "No. I said it's okay," he told her, and he meant it. Thanks to his little Angel, peace filled his heart.

*****

By Sunday, Daniel was really missing Angel, so he decided not to wait until the following Friday to visit with her. He spent all day Monday and Tuesday sending out resumes to various tech companies. Tuesday evening, the day before Valentine's Day, he went shopping and bought a box of chocolates and a live, flowering plant. The next day, he planned on surprising Angel—not only with their usual strawberry milkshakes, but with the candy and flowers he'd bought. Of course, since he'd waited so long, he paid inflated prices for the gifts, but he didn't mind; Angel deserved only the best. He imagined the surprise on her face when he walked in the door of her room the next day.

*****

The next morning, Valentine's Day, Daniel's peaceful slumber was rudely interrupted by a ringing phone in the hours just before dawn. He rolled over and groaned. That had to be his mother calling, but why would she be trying to reach him so early? The need for sleep outweighed his curiosity, and he allowed the answering machine to do its job. By the time Daniel woke up and was ready to go, he did not feel the need to listen to the message. The flashing light could wait until he returned from his Valentine's Day love mission. He felt like cupid, riding the bus with his backpack loaded down with gifts and a flowering plant in his arms. The female passengers nodded in obvious appreciation of his symbols of affection, while some of the guys looked frantic. No doubt, a few of them had forgotten what day this was! Lucky for them, it was still early enough to line up for flowers and chocolates with all of the other last-minute cupids. Daniel was proud of his selection of a plant with rainbow-colored flowers. They would complement Angel's colorful wig, and she might even be inspired to share her story behind the rainbow of colors. He couldn't wait to see the expression on her pretty little face and hear her tinkling-bell-like giggle when he made his grand, cupid-like entrance.

*****

The bus driver patiently waited for Daniel to exit the bus with his plant and backpack full of chocolates and strawberry shakes.

He sprinted up the steps to the third floor of the hospice, fairly bursting with excitement over surprising Angel today. He pushed through the door at the top of the staircase and stopped dead in his tracks.

The nurses' station was right in front of him, and several adults, their faces wet with tears, turned to stare at him. Two of them Daniel recognized instantly from pictures Angel kept on her nightstand. Her parents gazed at him with wide, sad eyes. Her mom covered her mouth and began to sob, and her husband put his arm around her and pulled her close, whispering something in her ear that Daniel couldn't hear.

One of the nurses patted her shoulder, and another nurse took a tentative step in Daniel's direction.

"I tried to call—" she began.

But Daniel didn't wait around to hear more. He raced down the hallway in pursuit of answers to the painful questions filling his mind. He entered Angel's room and skidded to a stop, glancing around frantically in search of his little friend.

Her bed was empty, so he crossed the room and peeked inside the bathroom. It, too, was dark and empty. *Oh, God. Oh, God. No...* The same thoughts looped through his head.

He turned around and ran right into Angel's mother, who pulled him into her embrace. Her sobbing only confirmed his worst fears. His little Angel, his sweet, loving Angel was gone. How could it be? It was Valentine's Day, and he was supposed to surprise her with special gifts to show her how much he loved her. Shock was setting in.

"She passed away peacefully, during the night," Angel's mother told him.

Daniel choked on feelings of sadness and guilt. If only he had visited her last Friday, he would have seen her one last time. He felt like he was drowning under waves of regret, and he struggled to keep his senses afloat.

"She left a message for you," her mother said, pulling away to cross the room and pick up Angel's iPad. She returned and held it out to him. "It's on here. She said she wanted you to have it." The woman smiled through her tears. "She said you'd know the password to get in."

Daniel took the pink iPad and stared at it, trying to imagine how his little Angel had the strength and fortitude to think of him in her dying days.

"She also said it's very important that you listen to the messages and follow the instructions she left for you." She sighed. "I have no idea what she meant by all this, but she seemed to think you'd know, and she said for you to remember the pact you made."

Daniel took a step back, clutching the iPad like a life preserver in a rough sea. He couldn't handle any of this right now. He needed to hug his little Angel and tell her everything would be okay. Instead, he was clinging to her memory. As Angel's mother began sobbing again, Daniel lost all control. The flowering plant fell from his hand, and he dropped his backpack onto the linoleum floor. No doubt, the milkshakes had tipped over inside and would soon saturate the box of chocolates he'd bought. A nurse rushed into the room.

"Oh, my. Well, that's okay. We can clean this up," she murmured reassuringly.

For a fleeting moment, Daniel imagined how Angel would have reacted, how she would have stifled her giggles behind her hand, and how she would have probably found a way to lay the blame on him… But then the reality of losing her hit him full force, and blindly, he turned toward the door, needing to escape. He desperately needed to free his mixed feelings, but he knew he had to compose himself first.

Suddenly, he became aware of how selfishly he was behaving. This mother had lost her daughter, and yet, she'd taken the time to console him. How could he be so inconsiderate as to just rush out on the poor woman? How could she be so caring? She was Angel's mother, and caring was in her nature, but now it was Daniel's turn to express his care and love. He turned and wrapped Angel's mother in a warm embrace, imagining he was hugging his little Angel.

"I'm sorry," he said, as honestly and sincerely as he could. "I'm really very sorry for your loss."

"Thank you," she said. She pulled back to look up at him. "I have a feeling my little Angel was a huge influence in your life. I'm proud of her for forming a friendship with you. I think you both needed each other."

Daniel nodded awkwardly. "Yes, she did, and I think you're right. At least, I know I needed her." His voice broke, and he knew he had to get out of there before he lost it again. "I have to go…"

He left Angel's room for the last time, slowly shuffled toward the nurses' station, and then paused to briefly embrace Angel's father.

"I'm sorry," he murmured, before pulling away.

He looked toward the group of nurses. "Thank you for taking such good care of her. I…I'm sorry for making such a mess in there." He nodded over his shoulder toward Angel's empty room.

He then turned and pushed through the doors to the stairway and fled as quickly as he could, anxious to be alone in his grief.

*****

The bus ride home passed in a blur for Daniel. He stumbled into his lonely basement apartment, knowing he had to call his mother. He pushed the button on the answering machine, expecting to hear her voice. Instead, he had to relive the shock of the day. The message was from one of the nurses at the hospice. He recognized her voice but couldn't picture her in his mind. In any case, she expressed her regret for informing Daniel about Angel's passing on his answering machine. Her message was apologetic and caring. She hadn't wanted Daniel to face the sad news when he next visited the hospice.

Too late for that now, he thought, but then again, there was no easy way to hear such horrible news. He picked up the phone and called his mother to tell her what had happened.

"She's gone," he said, the moment his mom answered the phone.

The sound of her muffled sobs was enough to break Daniel's heart.

"I'm so sorry—for her and for you," she said. "Should I come over? Do you need me?"

Just the sound of her voice had helped calm him, and Daniel shook his head. "No. I appreciate the offer, but I think I need some time alone to collect my thoughts and figure out what to do next."

"I understand," she told him. "But please, Daniel, call me if you need me, okay?"

"I will," he promised her, before hanging up the phone.

He went into his tiny living room, still carrying Angel's iPad, and dropped down onto the couch. "Now what?" he asked himself. He felt lost, adrift, with nothing to anchor him in life.

He looked down at the iPad. Angel had said he'd know the password, and he did, but he took no satisfaction when he figured it out on his first attempt. Pinky came to life when he typed in the words "love on," and the device connected him to Angel once again. He stared at the screen in disbelief. Her pretty, little face smiled back at him in the first of what appeared to be a series of video clips. He reluctantly pushed play. He sat in silent awe as his little Angel came back into his life on the same day she'd left him.

Still, something about listening to her soft, angelic voice sent shivers throughout his body. It felt strange to think that her body was at peace, but her spirit was alive and active. Daniel had to replay the video several times before he could grasp the reality of her message. There was no talking back or asking questions or debating his or her sanity. He knew this was how she wanted their relationship to play out. Angel was in control, while Daniel was feeling totally *out* of control.

Angel's message was full of optimism, humor, and some regret for not being able to say, "love on" one last time. Daniel sat there in a perplexed state. She never missed an opportunity to toy with his feelings. She was using technology to remind him to keep his love switch turned on. He felt her presence surrounding him and had to tell himself he was listening to a pre-recorded message. Thank goodness, the first video clip was short. Angel must have known this weird communication link was going to freak him out.

The message she delivered eased some of his anxious feelings. She reassured him the video clips were pre-recorded over the last several weeks. She had been journaling their visits, and unbeknownst to Daniel, she had been planning *The Quest to Lovify the World*. He felt like a pawn in her love game, and "Queen Angel" was going to direct his future moves. Sure enough, she referenced a text document that was time sensitive. She instructed him to read it as soon as possible because he might only have a couple of weeks to help her mother plan her celebration of life.

Daniel slumped farther down into his chair. His emotions were melting his heart, especially after the last comment from Angel. She ended the video clip with a wink and a "love on," but Daniel was stuck on the reality of her memorial. He had to force himself to open the text document that was staring directly into his soul. Didn't Angel realize he was going to be in a very vulnerable state? He had just lost her, and now he was supposed to carry on like she was still here? Daniel felt trapped in a nightmare he would have to relive every time he accessed Pinky. As if the video clip was not spooky enough, Angel's words in the text document about ripped open his heart and confirmed his part in *The Quest to Lovify the World*.

LLN1.txt

Dear Danny-Boy; he read,

If you are reading these words, then our relationship has reached a crossroads. I guess you could say I have crossed over, and you have to choose your path. You can join me up here, if you desire, or you can stay where you are, and help create Heaven on Earth. I wish I could be there to hug and comfort you, and maybe I am. If you look over your left shoulder... Sorry, that probably wasn't very funny. I'm sure you are freaked out enough without me playing ghost games. You have to trust that I will always be there for you in spirit. All you have to do is think of me or any loved one or a lost pet in Heaven for that matter. We are always close to your heart when you summon us.

I hope you enjoyed the first video. I kept it short, just in case your nerves were a bit too rattled. I recorded messages, knowing my time was drawing near. I also wrote love letters. You might be curious why this document is called LLN1.txt (Love Letter Number 1). Hope you "love" the title, and as you can imagine, you will be reading more of these if you choose. I kept a journal of our visits on Pinky. I know... maybe I should have told you I was taking notes. My intentions were true, and you sincerely helped me formulate our plan for carrying out the love quest. It is "our plan," by the way. It is not something I selfishly cooked up.

You were destined to be part of this love quest the moment you walked into my room. In fact, you were destined to play the lead role the moment you were born. I hope you can accept this is part of your destiny. Of course, everyone possesses the wonderful and sometimes tempting gift of free will. If you choose to come along for the most amazing and the most important journey of your life, please say, "I do." Ha-ha, don't worry, Danny-Boy, I am not asking you to marry me. It's too late for that, but I am curious about what you had planned for me on Valentine's Day?

Daniel had to stop reading and gather his thoughts. He felt like he was sitting in her room and listening to her rambling on as she described her latest idea or theory on life and love. She'd written the love letter as though she was talking face to face with him. It was creepy and yet satisfying, in a comforting way. She must have known the impact this was going to have on him. His curiosity and his desire to reconnect with her pulled his attention back to the love letter.

I bet you were going to surprise me with flowers and maybe a strawberry milkshake or two? I can't imagine the shock you felt when you received the call. I asked one of the nurses to notify you. On Sunday, I overheard the doctors tell my parents that I might not make it through the week. I knew on Tuesday morning I wasn't going to make it to Valentine's Day. How ironic is that, Danny-Boy—your little, love Angel might have passed away on the big love day? I know it probably sounds like a child's prophecy, but maybe Heaven needed some "Love Angels" for some special deliveries on Valentine's Day. I am your "Love Angel," Daniel; I hope you know that by now. Oh, before I forget to write this down, I got you a special Valentine's gift that will keep on giving for the rest of your life. It is one of my favorite love quotes: "If you keep your heart open, love will always find its way in." Think about it, Danny-Boy. It's perfect for our love quest, and it could be helpful for attracting that special person back into your life—wink, wink.

Speaking of love quests and loving relationships, I need to explain a few things, and I also need to divulge a big secret. I think you will appreciate the explanation; unfortunately, the secret or my confession might shock you. Sorry to admit that in advance, but I think you deserve fair warning. You must feel like an innocent fish being repeatedly shocked by an electric eel. Oh, well, this shock therapy won't kill you, and you know what they say—if it doesn't kill you, it might make you stronger.

First of all, we need to agree on the rules of the game. It is a game, you know, Danny-Boy, because the love quest has to be playful and fun. However, the rules I'm about to share with you refer to our relationship and the pact we made in regard to the quest. There are only three rules, and they will be easy to follow. But I am warning you now, if you violate the rules and break our Pinky swear pact, then I will come back and haunt you like a ghost on a vengeful mission. I don't think you want me spooking you at every turn, do you, Danny-Boy? I would much rather be your loving Angel than a scary ghost. So here are the rules:

1. Confidentiality – Sorry, Daniel, but you can't tell anyone about our ongoing connection. In time, you will be able to share the quest with everyone in the world, but in the meantime, "mum's the word." Now, if my mom or your mom asks about the message I gave you, you can show them a letter that I wrote for you. It is meant for prying eyes, and it just says stuff like "I miss you," "I love you," "I'm sorry," "blah, blah, blah." You will find it in the text document file with the name "Letter for Daniel."

2. Trust – You have to trust me, Daniel. I haven't led you astray yet, but there might be times when you will question my plans, instructions, and sanity. I have tried to make the quest easy for you to follow. So, just like Dorothy in The Wizard of Oz, follow the yellow brick road, and you will arrive at a magical place.

3. Faith – You have to have faith in yourself and faith in the love quest. I know in my Angel heart you can do this. I realize your confidence and self-worth might be shaken by the past, but you, my loving Danny-Boy, are stronger than you realize. Faith will carry you through the self-doubt and the challenges that might arise along the way. You also need to have faith in something bigger than yourself. It could be God, the universe, or whatever rings true for you. As you know, I have a strong faith in God, and I see God as the ultimate teacher of unconditional love.

As you can see, the rules are simple, and they will help keep you on track in pursuit of fulfilling the love quest. I will be there for you, too, helping to guide and encourage you along. The first task and the first test of the rules will involve planning my celebration of life. Oh, I wish I could see the expression on your face right now. That's right, Danny-Boy; you are going to be part of my life's celebration! I hope you are comfortable with public speaking because I have selected you to read my eulogy. Before you make any excuses, please know I already told my mom about this request. She said she would honor my wishes, and she would support you. Daniel, I have tried to make it easy for you, as I prepared a draft eulogy. You are welcome to make some minor changes, but please don't leave out any of the good stuff. Remember, I will be watching over you from above, and lightning could strike at any time.

Okay, I know this is a lot to digest on an emotional stomach. We're almost done for today. The remaining video clips and text documents are time sensitive, and they can only be accessed on a specified date. Once they are opened, you can always go back to view my lovely smile or re-educate yourself with my wise teachings. Of course, if you try to be a keener and jump ahead, Pinky will self-destruct. Just kidding, Danny-Boy. Does it feel like you are starring in a Mission: Impossible *movie? Maybe I should have added a soundtrack for your entertainment? Just to be clear, you can only connect with me when I say. So now, it is time for questions. Ha-ha, I almost got you with that one.*

Seriously, though, Daniel, it is time for my confession and the unveiling of the big Angel secret.

Daniel finished reading about her big secret, and then he sat there motionless. He felt like he was stuck between two worlds. One world he thought he knew and one that stretched his imagination to the breaking point. He read her confession over and over again, but it just hurled him deeper into the unknown. How could this be true? Why would she say something so shocking? He tore himself away from the iPad and staggered into the bathroom. Nervously, he glanced into the mirror to see if there was a crazy person staring back. Mind blown, and his heart ripped wide open; *The Quest to Lovify the World* had officially begun.

The quest to be continued in Book II

If you are curious about book II and the origins of the "Quest" or if you want to learn more about *Luvffirmations* or if you want to help *light up the world with love,* please visit us at:

www.lovifytheworld.com

Love On!